My One and Only Knight
A Merriweather Sisters Time Travel Romance Novella
Book 4

Cynthia Luhrs

My One and Only Knight, A Merriweather Sisters Time Travel Romance Novella

Copyright © 2017 by Cynthia Luhrs

Acknowledgments

Thanks to my fabulous editor, Arran at Editing720
and Kendra at Typos Be Gone

For JW, for making me laugh.

Chapter One

June 21, 1999—Holden Beach, North Carolina

"Come on, Mildred, just try it. How do you know you don't like it unless you try?" Penelope "Pittypat" Merriweather eyed the red paint spattered on the ends of her hair before flicking the braid over her shoulder and waggling her brows, thoroughly enjoying her eldest sister's discomfort.

"I am not cavorting under a full moon buck naked with you and your weird friends." Mildred sniffed. The look on her face would turn the handsome knight, on a dangerous quest to win his lady's hand, to stone with one glance.

Penelope watched her sister out of the corner of her eye. "You know clothing is always optional. We don't mind if you're the only one wearing strategically placed scarves."

Instead of replying, Mildred made a face as if she'd smelled a dead skunk. Penelope laughed on the inside and pushed the cart up and down the aisles of the Harris Teeter, stocking up on last-minute essentials for the celebration tonight.

It was the summer solstice and a full moon—an auspicious sign, a time when she and her friends celebrated the ocean and sky, and gave thanks for everything good that had happened to them over the past three months. No matter what was happening in their lives, they celebrated every solstice on the beach. With a bag of green grapes in one hand and red in the other, Penelope mentally tallied how much food she needed for tonight. They'd be short three of the usual members; all three had family obligations and were out of town for several days. No matter—they'd be there for the next celebration.

"I think that's everything. We've got the olives and cut-up veggies, cheese and crackers, and Rainbow is bringing her famous fudge and Hello Dolly bars, so that just leaves the most important item on the list...the wine." She shivered in her shorts and t-shirt, which proclaimed, *I can't adult today*, while they went over the list standing next to the refrigerated case containing dairy products.

Mildred dug in the huge taupe purse she never went anywhere without.

"Hold on, I've got a coupon for twenty percent off a case." She looked at Penelope and winked. "Maybe they'll let us use it twice."

"Or three times." Penelope laughed, filling the second cart her sister pushed. As they debated what to pick for the third case, a nasal, high-pitched voice shattered the air.

"Look, Annie, it's that Merriweather woman."

Annie wrinkled her nose as if she'd stepped in dog poo. "You know what they say." She nodded to her friend.

"She'll steal your man while you're sleeping."

Mildred snapped her bag shut and scowled. "I've got this, Pittypat."

Oh boy, Mildred's left eyebrow was twitching, which meant one thing: she was fired up. When their youngest sister, Alice, was small she couldn't say "Penelope." Somehow "Pittypat" came out of her mouth instead, and it stuck. From then on, everyone called her Pittypat instead of Penelope, even though she'd long outgrown the childish nickname and preferred Penelope—not that anyone had ever listened, but when it came down to what really mattered, the Merriweather women were always there for one another.

"If you can't hold on to your man, he wasn't really yours to begin with, so it isn't really stealing now, is it?"

Mildred looked down her regal nose at the two women.

"By the looks of you two, I'm surprised you could catch a man, let alone keep one."

"Why I never." The woman gasped. "Come on, Annie, let's get out of here."

Annie tossed her rather orange hair. "Bless your heart, Mildred. Everyone knows no one will have a frumpy old thing like you, and while Pittypat sure can turn heads, she doesn't have a clue how to hold on to a man. Your sister would have better luck holding on to a pig covered in bacon grease." She sniffed. "Divorced eight times and never attends church." Annie, the town gossip, waggled a finger. "Better take care you don't stand too close, Mildred. Wouldn't want to get struck by lightning."

The women flounced out, and Penelope gently placed a hand on Mildred's arm. "Let them go. Who cares what they think. The Merriweather sisters forever. Right?"

"You're right." Her sister's nostrils flared, and she turned rigid, pushing the cart to the open checkout lane. As much as Penelope wanted to reach out and hug her sister, smooth away the hurtful words, it would only make Mildred bristle, so she kept a firm grip on the cart and her mouth shut.

The doors whisked shut behind the two busybodies, cutting off the ugly whispers as they left the grocery store. Mildred helped Penelope unload everything, and after being in the air conditioning, it was hotter than blue blazes outside. With the groceries safely stowed in the trunk and the overflow in Mildred's Caddy, Penelope hopped into her 1960 blood-red MG roadster, tying a scarf over her hair.

"See you at the house."

"Try not to break the sound barrier today," Mildred called out as she climbed into the white Cadillac and then sedately drove out of the lot.

A woman Penelope had met on a road trip through Colorado had sold her the MG. The lady said her husband had recently passed away, and since he'd been nothing but trouble, she offered Penelope the car for a hundred bucks. Talk about a steal: it had been lovingly restored, with modern features added, like a fancy heated steering wheel and seats, and lots of speakers for the radio. So Penelope sold her big Mercedes and drove the cute roadster home, top down the entire way.

Sunglasses on, Penelope roared out of the parking lot, a song about longing and love filling the air as she sped back to her sanctuary, laughing as the wind whipped and made her feel alive as the sun beat down. Mildred always told her the car was so tiny and close to the ground that she worried it wasn't safe, but Penelope would drive it until it fell apart. She loved every detail about the little car.

As she crossed over the bridge, Penelope relaxed. Almost home. The cottage sat at the far end of Holden Beach, dunes on the left and a huge house on the right, though the owner lived in Boston and only came to the beach a few times a year. He was in finance or something else high-pressured, and kept mostly to himself when he was in town, though Rainbow had a huge crush on the guy.

The street across from her was lined with rentals, though the folks staying there had to walk a bit to reach the public beach access, so lots of times she had the beach to herself. Her sister lived several rows back; her house overlooked the intracoastal waterway. It was nice being able to walk to each other's houses, though Mildred didn't really like to have people over, said they ruined the furniture, which always made Penelope giggle, since it was covered in plastic and hot as Hades to sit on in the summertime.

Penelope snorted as her sister rolled to a stop behind her.

"I leave before you and you still beat me here," Mildred said.

"Why do you think I donate so much money to the police?" As they carried the groceries up the steps into the kitchen, Penelope couldn't resist teasing, "Anyway, if I ever get in trouble, that hottie, Will, will let me go, since he has a huge crush on you."

Mildred sniffed. "Whatever."

Penelope let it go but couldn't keep the grin off her face. "What's so funny?"

"Just thinking about how different people are."

The wine landed on the counter with a thunk. "You know, Pittypat, you shouldn't egg them on."

"Come on, Annie and her friend should work for the CIA. They are the worst busybodies I've ever met."

"You have to admit, you purposely go out of your way to be outrageous with your solstice parties and the fact you work from home. They don't know what to make of you."

"I write copy for tons of companies, so I'm busier than most people, and anyway, it's not like I'm growing pot in the dunes. Let's take a break. Do you have a few more minutes?"

"Sweet tea?"

"With mint, just like you like it. Go on out and I'll pour." Penelope poured the tea into Mason jars, put on a mint-green crochet cozy for hers and a white one for her sister, and took them out to the porch, where they stretched out, listening to the waves hit the shore.

"Don't you want to be normal?" Mildred asked.

"Normal? What is normal? Something made up by a bunch of stuffy old bats. I'm me, normal or not, so who cares? Don't people have better things to do than worry about what I'm doing with my life? If they spent as much time on themselves, this world would be a better place." Penelope set the glass down hard enough to rattle the spoon.

Mildred rolled her eyes. "Can't you at least knock off the naked cavorting?"

"Honestly, if they don't want to see a bunch of women appreciating nature and shouting out our thanks, they shouldn't peep from behind the dunes."

Her sister threw up her hands. "I give up."

"Don't worry, Mildred, they know you're normal and I'm the weird one. You know that's why Alice left—she couldn't stand the small-town gossip."

"We will agree to disagree, I guess. Are they bringing the girls out for a week before they go back to school?"

Penelope sipped the icy tea feeling the salty air settle on her skin. "She said they'd all come the middle of August right before the girls go back to school. I'll put them up here."

"Good. Those girls are adorable, but goodness they make a mess." Mildred stood, smoothing her silver bob back into place. "Have fun tonight. Try not to make too much noise."

"I love you too, Mildred." Penelope hugged her sister tight, then went inside to work. There was a lot to do before the sun set.

Chapter Two

August 1305—England

Oakwick Manor smoldered in the deepening dusk, the flames melting into the red sky as Thomas Wilton watched the destruction of his family home. He absently patted his sister, Josephine, on the shoulder as she sniffled into his tunic, her sobs muffled by the cloth.

It was his duty in life to look after them, even if they were a product of his late father's adultery. No matter; family was family, and he would see them provided for the rest of their days. Without responsibility and honor, civilization crumbled, leaving the weak to be preyed upon by the wicked.

"There, there, Josephine. We will rebuild, better than before. Oakwick will rise again."

Her reply was muffled as he looked up to see his younger brother, Heath, striding toward them, hair mussed from running his hands through it—or, more likely, from staying up gambling and wenching all night.

"What the bloody hell happened?"

This set off a new round of wailing from Josephine. Thomas looked around, grateful to see the housekeeper. "Mrs. Lind, please take Josephine to the cottage."

"Yes, sir."

There was a small guest cottage on the grounds that had survived the blaze where they could spend the night until he found more suitable accommodations for everyone.

A servant said a candle fell, causing the blaze, but Thomas felt the wrongness of the tale in his gut. Not sure how he knew, only that he did, he turned on his heel and strode to the still-intact stables, Heath trailing behind him, complaining about his head aching.

"What—"

Thomas put a finger to his lips, and once they were deep in the stables, now quiet with the horses moved to safety, he cleared his throat.

"I do not believe 'twas an accident."

"The servants said a candle toppled and started the fire. You do not believe them?"

Thomas tapped his lip, thinking. His gut had served him well on the field of battle many times, and he would trust it now. "There are those who always seek to harm others— mayhap another wool merchant or a man sniffing after your sister, thinking he can steal her away. One of the stable boys saw a man watching Josephine a few nights ago."

"Don't worry, Tom. You know Jo; she has lots of suitors. You worry overmuch." Heath peered at him. "I know you think me lazy, wenching and drinking all day, but I am a man and can look after her. You have no reason to care for us." He cuffed Thomas on the shoulder. "I see you've a few new scars. Is it true, then?"

Instead of replying, Thomas arched a brow, waiting.

"Wallace was captured?"

He ran a hand through his dark hair, wishing for a bath that was hours away, if at all this night. "'Tis true. I saw it with my own eyes."

His brother whooped and raised a hand in the air. "Why aren't you happy?"

"It could have been my head going to the noose. The smuggling the past few years to get the wool trade up and running. Wallace is a warrior. In another life, I might have called the man friend."

"You need a cup of ale and a wench. You're maudlin. Too much fighting, not enough wenching." Heath laughed.

Thomas's brother had no responsibilities, happy to let life unfold as it would while he laughed and loved. Thomas had no time for love, which reminded him to search for a wife this year. Someone content to run his home while he handled business and fought in tourneys, building up his fortunes. If they suited and did not argue overmuch, he would be content. He did not begrudge the children of his father's dead mistress their joy, only wished he might find a reason to laugh again.

Since his parents had been killed in a carriage accident in London when Thomas was thirteen, he had taken his responsibilities for his family and his people seriously. Days like today, looking at the smoking ruins of his home, he wanted to run away and lose himself in battle, not worry about anyone but himself, laze about and grow fat while his children played in the sun and his wife took care of the estate and people, but not today.

Today he would see the two most important people in the world—not bastards but Wiltons, and Wiltons always took care of those who belonged to them, to the cottage. Then he would make arrangements for rebuilding to begin, ensure his servants had somewhere to sleep. Then, and only then, would he have a bath, scrape the grime off his weary body, and enjoy a cup of ale.

Chapter Three

A group of curious gulls bobbed their heads in time with the drums, and a few sang along to the violin as Penelope and the others danced under the light of the full moon, the ocean glittering like black crystals where the light caressed the water. The sound of the waves pulsed through her as she swayed back and forth, grateful to live on the water, surrounded by friends, and happy...or maybe content was a better word. Only one thing was missing from her life. The mate to her soul.

A distant rumble had her looking up, and when she looked back down, her shadow had deserted her, the only remaining light coming from the houses further down the beach. The moon was banished by the clouds, and the wind wailed through the grass on the dunes, adding a discordant note to the night's festivities. Rain fell, gently at first, then stinging as thunder rumbled closer like a herd of horses galloping across the sky, and lightning imprinted itself on the back of her eyelids.

There were shrieks and laughter as the music stopped and the women ran for the house, scattering the gulls. The women's tan bodies, illuminated by the frequent flashes of lightning, stood out in stark relief against the storm. There was a huge basket waiting by the door filled with monogrammed towels, and each woman grabbed one, drying off. They were soaked, but as no one wore any clothes, it was only their hair that dripped on the floor, leaving tiny pools of seawater. They all wound towels around their heads, looking like part of a multicolored harem of some long-lost sultan.

"There's another basket in the bedroom for your wet towels. Go on and change into comfy clothes while I pour the wine."

"Red for me," Rainbow said. Several others called out red or white, and a few wanted St. Germain and bubbly, a summertime favorite here at Gull Cottage.

Penelope tossed her towel in the laundry room and pulled on a red silk caftan. She quickly wound her long sable hair into a French twist, noticing the gray. She'd been lucky: all the Merriweather women turned gray early, some as young as twenty, others in their forties, but they all ended up a beautiful silver, unless they circumvented nature and visited their hairdresser to try and hold back time.

With a smile, she touched the light strands as she wove in chopsticks to hold the twist. Then, after washing her hands, she stood in front of the floor-to-ceiling shelves and tapped her lip with a forefinger. The seagull dishes would be perfect for tonight—the image of the dancing gulls made her grin.

She'd found the dishes at an estate sale, the delicate blue edged in gold with the mischievous white bird in the center. By now her friends were used to eating on china—her oldest set was from her great-great-grandmother, was over two hundred years old, and yes, she used them even for something as simple as pizza. What was the use of having china if one let it sit in a cabinet unloved? Out of the eight sets of china, the Haviland was the only one she had to hand-wash; the rest could go in the dishwasher. The heavy lead crystal wine glasses were from Edinburgh Crystal. It was sad they were no longer in business. She fondly remembered her trip to Scotland and going behind the scenes at the factory to etch a tumbler. It sat in the cabinet, perfect for a hot toddy in the winter.

As the women emerged out of the bedrooms, dressed and chatting, they helped set out the food, everything from cucumber sandwiches to moon pies, and Pepsi for those that didn't care for wine or champagne.

"Oh my goodness, did you hear? Laura Ann left her husband." One of the women leaned against the counter, a glass of red wine in hand.

"I heard she left him for the pool boy, twenty years younger than her." Rainbow smirked. "Have you seen her pool boy? He could double for a young Keanu Reeves." She sighed dramatically, sending them all into discussions of which leading men they'd want to star alongside.

"Well, I'd make a list and demand my agent land me parts where I got to smooch each one," another added. They cackled, sprawled out across the white slipcovered sofas, blue and white floral chairs, and multicolored oversized floor cushions as they caught up on the latest gossip.

"These little quiches are amazing. I have to get the recipe."

Penelope nodded to the woman, a newcomer not only to the group but to Holden Beach. "I'll text it to you before you leave tonight."

Talk turned to wine and books and, of course, the men in everyone's lives, and how difficult it was to date in one's thirties and beyond.

"So when are you getting married again, Pen?" Rainbow waggled her eyebrows.

"Isn't nine the charm?" another teased.

One of the blonde twins chimed in, "Nine? Why not go for a baker's dozen?"

They all laughed as Penelope smiled. Let them tease her—at least she had the courage to keep trying. Certain her one and only love was out there somewhere, she didn't care how old she was; she'd keep searching for him no matter what. For all she knew, they'd passed each other and hadn't realized, waiting for the universe to bring them together at the right time. No matter what, love was truly all that mattered. Let responsibility and duty hang: she'd always choose love first. Who cared if true love was a fairy tale? She still believed.

"Where's Mildred?" one of the women asked, pulling Penelope out of her daydreams.

Rainbow answered for her: "She thinks we're a bunch of silly women who not only drink too much but are exhibitionists. She'll never join us."

"Plus she likes to be in bed by ten, and we don't get

started until midnight," Penelope added gently. Her sister was set in her ways, but she always meant well, somehow lacking the social gene that told her when she said something inappropriate or insensitive. While she could be awkward and standoffish, she had a big heart, and with Alice, their youngest sister, so far away and busy raising three girls, Mildred was all Penelope had. But her oldest sister detested children. Penelope was sure Mildred was going to make the perfect grouchy old lady.

And her? She liked children in theory, but she'd never felt the maternal urge her friends talked about even when she'd held babies. They smelled nice—well, when they weren't spitting up or pooping up a storm—but she didn't get the attraction. Maybe if she'd had a babe of her own, things would be different, but given she was thirty-nine, she was pretty sure her time had passed. And that was okay—no regrets, no matter what. That was her mantra, and it had gotten her through tough times, so she saw no reason to think otherwise.

Rainbow was the first to stand up and stretch. "I've got to be up early for court tomorrow. Can I help you clean up?"

Penelope shook her head. "It's no trouble. Go on home while there's a break in the storm."

The others put their glasses on the counter and dishes in the sink, collecting their bags and hugging each other goodbye. Thunder rumbled across the sky as Penelope looked outside, watching the clouds blot out the moon again.

"Better hurry—looks like we're in for another round."

She waved goodbye to her friends, happy they had celebrated the summer solstice together. Lightning lit up the water, and without thinking about it, she walked barefoot down the stairs of the worn wooden walkway, down to the sand, still warm from the heat of the day.

Walking in the rain and during a storm was one of her favorite things to do. The moon kept playing hide and seek behind the clouds as they drifted across the sky, like mascara-covered cotton balls.

Wrapping her arms around herself, she stared at the water, inky black, the scent filling her nose and making her skin tight, and sent up a plea.

"I keep trying to get it right. Please, universe, send me my match, a man I can love, mind, body, and soul. A great love I'll never forget."

The wind blew, and she inhaled deeply, turning her face up to the sky, tasting the rain on her tongue. It was salty, and as the wind tugged her down the beach, Penelope swore she smelled metal and leather, which was odd. Salt, sand, and the smell of suntan lotion mixed in with the ocean air were what she usually smelled, but tonight was different. As she stood staring at the water, pondering where the smell could be coming from, lightning struck the sand close enough to make her jump.

The skies opened up, the wind whipping, blowing sand into her face, stinging her arms and face. For a moment she swore she saw silver eyes in the clouds, and even more disconcerting? She was sure she saw a sword fall into the ocean. But that was ridiculous. It wasn't a moment after she'd taken one step into the water to investigate that thunder shook the beach, making her change her mind. No matter; she'd come back in the morning. And with that,

Penelope ran for the house, the wind tearing the chopsticks from her hair as it streamed out behind her, the red caftan a beacon in the darkness.

As lightning struck so close she could smell the ozone in the air, Penelope grabbed the wood post, cutting the side of her thumb. Another bolt lit up the night sky, illuminating one crimson drop that fell in slow motion and was swallowed by the sand. Making a mental note to call the handyman to fix the nail sticking out, she sprinted across the worn boards and into the dry, cozy house.

Chapter Four

Thomas had stopped by the cottage to see how Josephine and Heath fared in their small quarters. Though his sister had assured him they were more than comfortable, he hadn't liked leaving them, even as he posted two guards to watch her at all times in case there was truth to the rumor of a man looking to steal her away.

During the day, he had purchased several horses. The stables were untouched, so there was plenty of room for the animals, thanks to the quick thinking by the stable boys. Tired and hungry, he pushed open the door, blinking at the dim interior after the bright afternoon light. The inn reeked of men and ale; unwilling to linger, Thomas ate fast, though when he passed by a group of men, some voice within warned him, and he avoided the man's booted foot.

"Apologies, fine sir."

Without bothering to answer, Thomas threw open the

door and inhaled, ridding his nose of the odors as he walked across the courtyard to fetch his horse. Later he'd wonder what made him hesitate, the same sense that warned him in battle. If this had been a battle, his head would be lying at his feet looking up at him. The blow came from behind —"Cowardly whoresons," he uttered as he dropped to his knees and landed face first in the muck.

When Thomas came to, he was trussed up like a boar, rolling back and forth in the back of a rather shabby carriage. Scuffed brown boots, the same he saw when he fell, were inches from his nose. Following the boots up, he flinched.

"How can it be? I watched you fall. Quick, cut me loose and we will end these bastards."

The man he'd called comrade, friend, sneered.

"You left me in that godforsaken land to die."

"I thought you dead, would not have left you behind in Jerusalem if there was slightest chance you were alive."

"Yet here I am. Am I a ghost come to haunt you, perchance?"

Realization dawned. "Hugh, Grant, and Robert. 'Twas you."

The carriage came to a stop, the door opened, and he was roughly grabbed and tossed onto the ground.

"They found out I was stealing the gold for myself. I had no choice but to kill them. Now there are none left except you and I. The gold will pay for repairs to my estate. I am in debt; money does not go so far as it used to, and women with large dowries are even harder to come by." He kicked Thomas in the gut. "Soon you will join your brothers in arms."

But while Roger had been blathering on, Thomas slid the

blade from his boot—idiots hadn't bothered to check him for weapons other than his sword, and it would cost them dearly. The last of the ropes fell free, and he rolled, coming up in a crouch, teeth bared, knife slashing downward.

Four men rushed him while the coward he once called friend stood back, arms crossed over his chest, watching the spectacle. One fell as Thomas's blade opened the man from shoulder to elbow. Striking again, Thomas lunged for the fallen man's sword and thrust up behind him as he knelt, the sound of the man's strangled cry telling him his aim was true.

Pain sliced through his back as the blade bit down. The next blow came to his thigh, and he roared and spun to face his remaining two attackers, sword and knife at the ready, blood streaming down his arms and legs. He wiped the scarlet from his eyes as thunder crashed across the sky.

In the next instant, the two men lunged, and hell was unleashed upon the very earth he stood upon as the ground rumbled and bucked, sending one of the men to his knees as the most ferocious storm Thomas had ever experienced swept across the land with a vengeance. Thomas leapt into the air with a battle cry, sword raised high, and aimed for Roger's neck—they collided, the earth gave way, and they fell.

Thomas spat out seawater as another wave crashed over him. The skies turned black, and the wind whipped, sending water into his eyes and nose as he struggled to keep his head above the churning waves. As a boy he had heard tales of a terrible storm such as this when sea monsters came forth to drag ships and men to their doom.

A wave drove him under, and he choked, his injuries burning in the water, and then there was a bump against his leg, the feeling of something large. As he was pulled under, he struggled to strike at the foul monster dragging him to his death, but it was fast, and the deeper it pulled him, the more his vision dimmed as Thomas struggled to reach the other blade in his boot. Deeper and deeper the beast took him as he looked up and swore he saw sunlight break through, sending a beam down through the darkness to save him.

Chapter Five

The dull ache woke Penelope. The cut on the fleshy part of her thumb was red around the edges, and throbbed in time to her heartbeat. After a quick text to the handyman to take a look at the railing, she padded to the bathroom. Nothing like a hot shower to get the day started off right.

A spot of blood from her thumb appeared on the towel, and she sucked on the cut while she searched for a bandage, coming up with a dusty character from a kids' TV show, left over from the last time her nieces visited. It would be lovely to see them again before the summer was over—her sister and family were so busy with work and the kids' activities that they rarely had time to visit anymore.

Jennifer Lopez sang her heart out as Penelope sang along. Dressed and finished with her cup of green tea, Penelope gathered her hair into a ponytail and stretched in pleasure when the sun hit her skin, the smell of the ocean making her feel that all was right in the world as she padded across the worn wood, sighing when her bare feet touched the warm sand.

After the intense storm last night, she was eager to see what might have washed up. Sometimes Penelope found a beautiful shell or rock, and occasionally a piece of sea glass. The sunrise turned the sky into a pastel abstract painting, making the perfect time for a walk, with no crowds out and about this early. At this end of the beach there were never many people, with the dunes to the left of her, and to the right an enormous house that was only used a few times a year when the owner, who lived in Boston, was able to get away from his high-powered finance job. When he was in town, she'd see him pacing on the deck on his phone the entire first day of his arrival, but by the time he'd decompressed, it was time for him to go back.

The sun warmed her bare shoulders as she meandered along, wearing a red sleeveless shirt and gingham shorts, stopping occasionally to look at an interestingly shaped piece of driftwood. A bit further down the beach she noticed someone had left their blankets out last night, and they were covered in sand. As she got closer, a sound had her turning to locate the source. It was coming from the blankets, and she hesitated. The noise came again, blending with the waves and the call of a raven. The black bird landed on the lump, and it moved, causing the bird to investigate. As a corner of the cloth blew back, Penelope spied long, dark hair and broke into a run, the shells she'd collected falling to the sand, forgotten.

Scanning the horizon, Penelope didn't see any signs of a

shipwreck, and a scan of the beach around her didn't help either. There wasn't anything out of the ordinary—well, except for a person on the beach moaning.

Were they ill? She'd knelt down, her hand outstretched to touch the person, when she noticed it was a man under the tattered blanket, dressed in a tunic-type shirt and formfitting pants—almost like leggings, but there were rips in the clothing, not just at the shoulder and arm but his back and thighs.

"Hello? Are you sick?" Penelope spoke loudly, but he didn't stir. Some of the people renting a house for the week tended to overindulge and sometimes fell asleep on the beach, but him...his clothes looked old, not like a homeless person, but museum old. There was something odd going on.

When she shook his shoulder, he grunted but didn't wake. Annoyed he might be sleeping off a hangover, she rolled him over, gasping when she saw his face.

It was harsh, battered, and bruised, and yet, even with the injuries, he was so beautiful that a sculptor would have fallen to his knees and wept, thanking the heavens above for sending him such a promising subject.

Silvery eyes the color of the sea during a storm, framed by the longest lashes she'd even seen outside of falsies, fluttered open.

"Bloody hell."

"I'll say. How much did you have to drink last night?"

He spoke, the rapid words filling the air but not making any sense as her brain struggled to identify and then translate the language.

"Sorry, my French is pretty rusty."

The man cleared his throat, which brought on a coughing fit. She quickly pushed him onto his side as he retched up seawater, helpfully pounding him on the back until he was done.

"Where am I, demoiselle?" he said as she helped him sit up, her eyes traveling over him, noting the wounds. Was he an escaped felon?

"The salt water washed your wounds clean."

He looked down at his bicep, the jagged gash. "Four against one—five if you count Roger." He peered at another cut on his washboard stomach that looked like someone had mistaken him for a loaf of bread. "'Tis naught but a scratch."

The man made a strangled noise in the back of his throat, pointing at the houses hugging the beach, his mouth opening and closing, almost as if he'd never seen a house before. Those beguiling eyes were filled with panic as he gripped her arm.

"Am I in hell, then? Are you a demon come to take me to the depths of the fiery pit?"

"I've heard Holden Beach called a lot of names over the years, but never hell." She pulled him up, glad he staggered to his feet—given his size, she would have never managed on her own.

"Come on, let's get you inside and cleaned up. Then you can call... Is there someone who can come get you?"

He stumbled, and Penelope summoned every bit of strength to keep him from falling, exhaling with relief when he found his balance. The man kept turning his head from side to side, as if he'd never seen a beach before. Maybe he hadn't.

"I fear I have traveled a great distance. This does not look like Dover."

"As in England?"

The man nodded, reaching out to touch the grass growing around the dunes.

"Goodness' sakes, how much did you have to drink? You're in Holden Beach." At his blank look, she elaborated. "North Carolina?"

Nope. Nothing. Either this guy was good, or he'd taken a hit on the noggin.

"America?"

But he shook his head, turning paler by the moment. They were almost to the walkway, and she hoped he'd make it, otherwise she'd have to call the paramedics to move the big lug.

"I do not know this place, mistress."

"Watch out—"

But it was too late—he'd grabbed the railing with the nail sticking out. He looked at the blood welling on his palm then wiped it on his tunic with a shrug.

"I've got someone coming to fix that later today."

The man she'd half carried in from the beach sat in her kitchen, gaping at his surroundings as if he'd never seen a modern kitchen before. While she watched, he ran his hands through his hair, wincing and looking a bit green around the edges.

"You've got quite a bump there."

"Aye. The bastard struck me with a sword."

Sword? What on earth? "You must be suffering from memory loss. Let's try something. What's your name?"

"Thomas Wilton, lady."

"I'm Penelope Merriweather, but my friends call me Pittypat."

He looked at her, eyes boring into her as if seeing her for the first time since she'd found him, his gaze lingering on her lips before traveling down to her coral-painted toes, turning on a furnace inside her. As she watched him, he jumped and darted another glance at her toes, pointing.

"Penelope is a beautiful name." He hesitated. "Why do your feet bleed, lady?"

She couldn't help the smile that spread across her face.

"They're not bleeding—it's polish, to make them pretty." Where on earth had this guy come from? Had the bump to his head left him thinking he was actually some kind of historian or medieval knight?

"You know your name, so I don't think it's memory loss. Let's try a bit more. Where are you from?"

"Dover, England."

"Good, how about family? A wife?"

He opened his mouth to answer just as the phone rang, and the poor guy jumped a foot in the air, landing in a crouch, hand going to his hip, eyes wild.

"My sword, where is it?" He patted his boots. "My blades are gone as well. Did you take them?"

"No." She looked for the ringing phone, lifting up piles of mail on the counter until she found it.

"I didn't see any sword or blades on the beach. You must've lost them last night. Shouldn't drink so much." She held a finger up. "Hold on, let me answer this."

As she talked to her sister, Thomas watched her mouth,

his gaze ping-ponging between her lips and the phone at her ear, making her self-conscious.

"Pittypat, I try not to meddle in your foolishness, but you need to listen to me: that man could be homeless, crazy, or some kind of escaped convict. There's no sense in borrowing trouble. I'm calling the police."

"No, don't, Mildred. He just hit his head pretty hard, and I think he's suffering from a short-term delusion, thinks he's some kind of medieval knight. You know I hate hospitals; that's where sick people go and don't come back. Anyway, he isn't sick—with a few days of rest he'll remember he's a stockbroker or doctor, or maybe a construction worker, by the build on him."

There was a heavy sigh before Mildred replied, and Penelope could picture her sitting in the outdated harvest-gold kitchen, a giant cup of coffee at her elbow as she twisted her long necklaces through her fingers over and over again.

"This isn't a stray dog or cat. He is a living, breathing man, and he could hurt you."

Penelope held up a hand as if she could reach through time and space and stop her sister from talking.

"I'm fine. Once I figure out who his family or friends are, I'll call them to come get him. And I'll see if Mr. Boston is in town this weekend. I didn't notice anyone next door, but this guy looks like he could be one of his friends."

But Mildred wouldn't hear it, and she started in on one of her rants. Instead of suffering through it, Penelope simply hung up with a sheepish grin at the man watching her through hooded eyes.

He sat transfixed a moment before shaking his head, then

he stalked over to her as if she were a piece of bread and he was a hungry seagull, took the phone from her hand, and examined it, running his fingers over the device, turning it over and over before holding it to his ear and then close to his mouth.

"Hello?" He frowned and shook the phone. "The strange box, what is it? You spoke into it. I heard a woman's voice answer you."

"It's a phone. Check your pockets—do you have one on you?"

The man again gave that blank look, so she slowly stepped beside him and gingerly touched his hips, looking for pockets. And, truth be told, she thoroughly enjoyed the muscles that rippled and flexed under her touch. Land's sake, he was like warm stone.

"That's odd, you don't have any pockets. I would've thought you'd have pockets at least in your pants."

She stepped back and looked at him again, this time more closely, noting faded scars through the tears in his shirt and pants. This was a man who'd lived a hard life.

"Oh well, it doesn't matter. It would've been ruined from the ocean anyway."

"Lady, you spoke to another person through this device. What kind of magic is this? Are you a witch?" He took two steps back from her, and she resisted the urge to start chanting lines from the Scottish play.

"Well, there are some people who call me a witch, but not the kind you're thinking of. I love celebrating nature, marking the change of the seasons, but can I cast spells?" She shook her head. "Don't I wish, but no, I can't. Come on, let's get you in the shower, and then I'll see about finding you some clothes. I think Rainbow's brother left a set last time he was here."

Chapter Six

How had he ended up in this strange land called America? The beautiful woman had found him senseless on the beach, and at first Thomas thought she was a mermaid come to take him back to the depths. Instead, the woman with eyes the colors of emeralds had shown him to a soothing room where she showed him wondrous things.

He caught sight of himself in the looking glass and peered closely, the reflection so clear that he spent overlong looking at himself, thinking he had never known what he truly looked like until this moment.

Had he always looked so fierce with his many scars and imperfections? Thomas rested his hands on the cold thing she called "sink" as he opened his mouth wide, looked at his teeth, and tilted his head back, trying to see up his nose.

Oakwick Manor was a smoldering ruin, and Josephine and Heath would be looking to him to rebuild and care for them. He had to make his way home, but with no funds to speak of, he needs rely on Mistress Merriweather. With him missing, Heath would try to take his place, but would soon tire of the duty and go back to wenching and drinking until there was no more gold.

After showing him how to make the water flow, Penelope had left him in the bathing chamber, saying again she was no witch, but he doubted her word after watching her summon forth blissfully hot water with a flick of her wrist.

He tried it now, turning the metal handle and jumping back when water splashed into the sink. In a moment it was hot, and he turned it off, turning on the other one, which was icy cold. Every time he caught sight of himself in the mirror, he jumped, which was unlike him, for Thomas was afraid of nothing except sea monsters and witches, but everyone was afeared of them if they cared for their mortal souls.

The water in the low bowl was still, and he put his hand in, surprised how cold it was. She had called it a toilet. There was a lever on the side he was supposed to push when he had relieved himself. Tentatively, he reached out and pushed the button, leaning close to watch the water swirl around and vanish, only to be replenished. Several times he pressed the lever and watched the water before relieving himself, though afterward he made sure to put the lid back down when he finished, as that seemed to be important to her, though in truth he wasn't sure why it made a difference.

The brush for his teeth was made of a material he had never seen before, smooth and shiny and bendable. What was the word? Plastic. He washed his hands and picked up the brush, eyeing the blue color doubtfully. There was no room for hesitation—she had been kind to him, but Thomas knew he had to quickly adapt to this strange place, convince her to aid him so he could go back home. As much as he wished to stay and explore this wondrous land and learn more about her, he had a duty, and he would see it done. What he wanted did not matter.

The sticky blue liquid that went on the brush for his teeth smelled like mint from the gardens, but why was it blue? He squeezed the tube, and the ointment went soaring through the air to land on the sink and mirror. By the third try, he had a mound on the brush, and, squaring his shoulders, put it in his mouth to clean his teeth. It felt strange in his mouth, but his teeth were smooth, and he rather liked how they felt.

Where was her husband? Mistress Penelope had not mentioned a man, and he had seen no sign, but how could she live alone? Mayhap she was a wealthy widow—the bathing cloths were thick and soft, unlike anything he had ever seen, and she had an overlarge stack of them for his use, yet no servants.

The tattered remains of his tunic and hose lay on the cool white floor, no longer fit for anything but the rag bin. The shower was another marvel, the water so hot that steam filled the chamber. Thomas groaned in pleasure as the heat eased his aches. His wounds no longer burned, aided in healing from the seawater.

There was a long shelf in the water chamber with many bottles with exotic names, each one smelling nicer than the next. The thing called shampoo, she said, was for washing his hair, and the one called shower gel was for his body. He didn't know why he needed two different ones, but he took her word. The shampoo said Coconut Delight, and as he smelled it, he thought he now knew what a coconut smelled like, even if it looked rather ugly and hairy on the image. He dumped a bit in his hand and frowned, not sure if it was enough, so he added more until his hand was overflowing. The resulting foam told him he had used too much, and his eyes watered as the liquid ran into his eyes, nose, and mouth.

When he'd finished scrubbing his hair, Thomas squirted the orange-scented shower gel into his hand. The smell filled the room as the steam from the shower made him feel like he had died and gone to heaven. He lingered overlong under the spray, marveling at how the water came from the pipes, but it finally started to turn warm and then cold, so he reluctantly dried off, wrapping the towel around his waist, one more task to tend to.

There was a can called "shaving cream" along with a pink instrument with two small blades. Eyeing the small blade dubiously, he shook the can and pressed the top, the resulting amount overflowing his hand, landing on the sink, mirror, and floor.

"Bloody hell," he yelped, jumping back. With another curse, Thomas cleaned up the best he could, smeared another handful of foam on his face, and held up the tiny pink blade, squinting at it.

"How hard could it be?" He knew later, as he stood looking at himself in the mirror, peering at the five small cuts on his face, that it would take him some time to get used to using the small instrument. There was a knock at the door, and he opened it.

"I wanted to tell you how to use the— Oh my, let me get

you some tissue paper." Penelope pulled a square from the roll next to the toilet, tore it into pieces, and stuck them on his face. "There, it'll stop the bleeding." Then she stepped back, her eyes huge as she took him in.

"I'll just leave you to get dressed." She ducked out the door and turned around, handing him a stack of clothing. "These belonged to a friend's brother, and I think they'll fit. He's in the military and isn't home very often, but he always keeps a change of clothes here when he stops by to recharge his soul at the beach."

She looked at him again, and Thomas thought of England, counted sheep—anything to forget the look of interest on her face so he would not embarrass himself in front of her.

The door shut, and he let loose a low, throaty chuckle. She found him pleasing and well formed. He would like to bed her— she had the lush curves a man could hold on to through the cold winter nights; she was the kind of woman he would go to war for, to keep for his own.

Dressed in the formfitting soft pants and shirt, he found her on the sofa. Once again he was struck by the view in front of him, the waves seeming to start right outside of her window.

"I thank you for aiding me in the use of the wondrous bathing chamber."

His stomach growled, and she put down a book, blinking at him, the corner of her mouth twitching.

"Wow, those won't do at all. And by the sound of your stomach, you're starved." She stood up, and he admired her form, the long dress concealing and revealing as she moved.

He swore he could watch her forever and not call the days wasted. If only he did not have the heavy mantle of duty calling him home.

"Let's go to the store and find you something better to wear, and then we'll get something to eat. You like pizza, right?"

Chapter Seven

Penelope wanted to fan herself after getting an eyeful when she barged in on Thomas in the shower. The broad expanse of chest, the heavily muscled arms and legs, the scars, new and old—whatever his history, it had been violent. But she did the nice thing and averted her eyes—well, she did sneak in a couple more glances here and there. After all, what red-blooded woman wouldn't with that kind of beauty in her bathroom?

"My wounds are almost healed. 'Tis faster than they have ever healed."

For a moment she heard the words, but they didn't register; she was busy looking at his washboard abs. Then she shook herself. "If you were in the ocean a long time, maybe that's what did it."

He shuddered.

"What?" She watched him closely, hoping he was having a

breakthrough, remembering something about himself or his family.

"In the water, during the storm, I felt a sea monster bump me before taking me down to what I thought was my watery grave, where it would swallow me whole if I was lucky, or tear me to shreds and feast on my entrails."

"Yuck, that's a disgusting image I won't easily get out of my head anytime soon." She pursed her lips. "More likely it was a shark or a curious octopus. Lucky you, it wasn't hungry. But you know...it might have been nothing more than a piece of debris from the boat you were on."

"Nay, I went over the cliff, took Roger with me. At least that useless lackwit is dead." He grinned at her. "It was a sea monster."

"I hate to burst your bloodthirsty bubble, but how can you be sure he's dead? After all, you survived."

"Bloody hell, I pray the bastard is dead," he muttered, and when his stomach rumbled again, she jolted out of her daydreams of having him around...for, well, a while. She led him out the front door and down the steps to the car. He eyed it uncertainly.

"We go in this? Where are the horses?"

"Guess you still think you're some kind of medieval knight? There are no horses. This is a horseless carriage; it goes on gasoline, liquid food. Get in—she doesn't bite."

He stood still, not moving as she got into the car, and when he still hadn't moved, she reached over and unlocked the door. As Thomas gingerly settled himself in the seat, she wanted to laugh. It was like a clown car with fifty clowns compressed inside; he took up all the space, making the car feel a tenth its size.

"It's a good thing it's nice out today. I'll put the top down."

She started up the engine of the MG, and he jumped, clutching the dash.

"Saints, what is that foul noise?" His hand went to his side again, and for a moment she wondered if he was telling the truth—he really thought he always carried a sword. It was something she needed to think about.

Top down, she turned in the seat to look at him. There was sweat above his lip, and he was pale, eyes rolling around like a nervous horse, and she thought for a moment he might be sick. Penelope placed a hand on his arm, and when he turned his face to hers, she held his gaze.

"You're safe, I promise. This is how we get from place to place. It may sound loud, and we're going to go quite fast, but I promise you, I've got your back."

He swallowed and, with a tight nod, turned his gaze to the interior of the car. Catching sight of her seatbelt, he frowned, reached for his own, and after a few tries managed to buckle himself in.

"Ready?"

He nodded. "Aye, lead on, lady."

"Please call me Penelope."

"As you wish, la—Penelope."

Maybe she should have called Mildred to drive them. Penelope had to keep telling herself to drive slower, as she had a well-deserved reputation around Holden Beach for having a heavy foot. Thank goodness it was only a fifteen-minute drive to the shopping center, because he held on as if he were afraid she was going to jump the car off the bridge or execute a roll and send him flying to his death.

They pulled into a parking spot. Thomas remained seated, his knuckles white, the tendons in his hands standing to attention, so quietly she went around and opened his door, offering her hand, which he clasped as if it were a life preserver thrown to a drowning man. Guess she really needed to work on slowing down a bit.

"You sure you're not going to throw up?"

His hand was clammy, but he squared his shoulders. "A Wilton does not swoon. 'Tis the motion of this horseless carriage; makes my entrails churn."

Deciding to keep quiet, she led him into the store and straight to the men's department. He did look ridiculous—the sweatpants were more like capri leggings, and the sweatshirt showed a tantalizing glimpse of his stomach, which made her feel like a teenager all over again, crushing on a good-looking guy in her classes.

"It's really hot this time of year, you'll probably want short sleeves and either shorts or lightweight pants." She led him over to a rack of golf shirts in a multitude of colors.

"There are so many to choose from." He touched the material, stroking the shirt. "'Tis such fine cloth. Where are the weavers?"

"They're in another country."

He looked pale again, then regained his equilibrium and sorted through the shirts, efficient in his movements, which she could appreciate, given how much she detested shopping.

Penelope reached in and held up an orange shirt to him.

The color was off, but... "I think you're going to need an extra large, based on your shoulders and chest." She had to tilt her head back to look up at him; she guessed he must be about six foot three to her five eight. The rack spun, and she reached in, pulling out an azure shirt that reminded her of the sky.

"Try this one—look for the XL on the tag."

As he moved to the extra-large shirts, she left him to pick out a few pairs of shorts. The weather app said it would be in the nineties and humid, so he'd be coolest in the shorts.

"Mistress Penelope?"

She popped her head above the rack. "I'm over here."

He walked over holding several shirts, and she caught the admiring gaze of two women as they walked by, arms laden with shopping bags. Narrowing her eyes, Penelope watched them until they were out of sight.

"Okay, I have no idea what size shorts you need, so try on a couple. I made my best guess." She handed him khaki, navy, and red in a couple of sizes.

"Where does the music come from?" He stood there blinking at her, and she pointed to the dressing room.

"From the ceiling. I'll explain later. Go in there where it says 'fitting room' and try this stuff on, see what fits."

He nodded at her, and as he walked into the dressing room, for a moment she felt like she was sending her kindergartner into the first day of school. He looked so forlorn.

While she waited for him to come out, she caught up on email, accepted three new copywriting requests, checked social media, and ignored the thirty-seven texts from

Mildred, instead answering an email from Alice. They had taken the girls to California for a week and were having a great time. She said they would be heading back, making the cross-country drive in a few days, and what had she ever been thinking to let the girls talk her into so much time together in a car?

Time passed, and Penelope looked toward the dressing room a few times, but there was no sign of Thomas. She was starting to worry when she heard a whisper.

"Mistress."

She walked over to see Thomas peeking around the corner of the dressing room.

"What's wrong?"

He beckoned her toward him, and she hurried due to the look on his face.

"I can't come in there. It's the men's dressing room."

"You must. There's something wrong." He made a strangled noise in the back of his throat, so with a quick look around, she stepped into the dressing room.

"Okay, I'm here. What's wrong?"

The door opened, and for a moment she lost all train of thought. Thomas smelled of the ocean, leather and pure male, and it took her a moment to place it, that unique combination of scents, but she did: the night of the storm. Had the universe granted her wish? And if so, was he truly from the past? No, that was fanciful, even for her.

The man in question was watching her, and there was an undeniable pull between them. He stepped forward.

"What are you doing in here? Honestly, what is with these couples today who can't keep their hands off each other for two minutes?" A man stood there, wearing a bright pink pair of pants, hands on his hips, glaring at them.

Thomas stepped around her. "Begone."

The man's eyes widened, and he fled the room, making her laugh.

"You'll have to teach me that. Might come in handy someday."

"I will send these weak men away." He chuckled, but the moment was broken.

"You look amazing."

She meant it—he looked like a model stepping off the pages of a magazine, a man's man obviously used to spending a great deal of time outside, and she must have been staring longer than was polite, because he made that sexy sound in the back of his throat again.

"I cannot wear these garments."

"Why not? They look fantastic."

"'Tis scandalous." He was looking at his bare legs in the mirror.

It was a challenge to keep the grin from her face. "It's what everyone wears. Trust me, you look fine."

He looked uncertain, but, seeing the look on her face, nodded. "If you say."

He headed back to the dressing room, and she stopped him with a hand on his forearm.

"Give me what you were wearing when you came in. I don't think you want to wear those out of here. After we pay for these, we need to get you a pair of loafers as well."

He kept the navy shorts and pale blue shirt on and gathered up the clothing he had worn, along with everything else, which she put back on the hangers.

"Wait, you need at least a couple more shirts and shorts."

He caught sight of the tag, turned it over, and blanched.

"'Tis so expensive, and I have no gold. Mine was lost in the storm."

She shook her head. "Don't worry about it. I'll take care of it."

He went back and forth between a couple of the shirts, and she could tell he liked three of them but didn't want her to spend the money, so she took all three from him with a firm shake of her head. "What did I say?"

He nodded and handed her three pairs of shorts to go with them.

The guy at the register looked up. "We'll take these, and here are the tags from what he's wearing." Then she stopped and looked back at the clerk. "Oh, where's the underwear?"

The man led them over to a rack behind him, and she motioned for Thomas to look.

"I'll just hold these at the desk—let me know when you're ready," the clerk said.

She absently nodded and pointed to the underwear. "I totally forgot. I'm sure you'll need some of these." She handed him a package, and he looked at her blankly. She pointed to the picture and then at him, and his face reddened again.

"Nay, I will not go around in those. Those are much too short, even for these things you call shorts."

She started to laugh, and the more she laughed, the funnier it became, until she was laughing so hard she was crying.

"No, you don't wear underwear by itself. They go under the shorts you're wearing."

He frowned and took the package from her, reading, his eyebrows going higher and higher until she could no longer see them. He handed the package back to her with a firm shake of his head.

"I will not wear such a tightfitting garment. I will go without."

She grinned at him. "Good choice. Going commando is always a good thing."

They went back to the clerk and paid for the clothing. Thomas insisted on carrying the bag for her.

"The shoes are over here. You'll need a pair of loafers—they're good for walking on the sand, and you won't be able to go into the restaurant wearing those ratty old flip-flops."

"Is that what they're called? They do make a sound when one walks."

She looked down at his feet, and thought that even his toes were perfect. In the shoe department, he quickly went from shoe to shoe, lovingly caressing them, smelling the leather.

"All of these? I can pick any of them?"

She nodded and showed him the loafers most of the men around Holden Beach wore. "These are really comfortable from what I've heard, and I think they'll look great on you."

"How long will it take to have them made?"

"They have them here in the store in the back. We just tell the clerk your size." She thought again how sad it was, whatever was going on inside his brain that he thought he was from the past. She was going to question him or over dinner, find out exactly from whence he thought he came, so to speak.

The salesclerk approached, sidling up to Thomas, and Penelope wanted to smack the drool from the woman's face, which was totally unlike her. She was really jealous over anyone.

"How can I help you today?"

Thomas handed her the shoe. "I require these."

"Okay, what size you need?"

He looked blank, and Penelope stepped in. "He'll need to be measured."

When the girl sauntered to the back to fetch the size thirteen shoes, Thomas sat there looking around, touching the chairs, looking at the lights and back to Penelope so many times that she knew he wanted to ask.

"They're electric lights. You flip a switch like in the bathroom at home, and they come on."

"But how do they come on?"

Penelope shook her head. "That's a discussion that's beyond me. When we get home, I'll sit you down in front of the computer and you can read about it to your heart's content."

The girl brought the shoes, and with a hopeful look waited around for a few minutes, but when Thomas dismissed her, she flounced back to the desk.

He stood and admired the shoes in the mirror. "These will do nicely."

"Good. Why don't you wear them home?"

Penelope took the box up to the clerk and paid her. "And could you throw these away?"

She handed her the ratty flip-flops, which the clerk accepted, wrinkling her nose.

As Penelope led him out of the store, she couldn't help but notice the glances women threw his way as they passed. He was an incredible-looking man, and so far he'd been exceedingly polite. She was determined to solve the mystery of Thomas Wilton.

Chapter Eight

Thomas's stomach growled yet again, so Penelope walked faster.

"I know, we missed lunch, but you're going to adore this pizza place." They detoured to make a stop at the roadster, where she stowed the packages in the trunk. As she straightened up, it all happened so fast: Thomas stepped away from the car as she screamed, "Look out!"

Heart pounding, sounds amplified, and the smell of burning tires permeating the air, she pulled Thomas back by the arm right before he would have been flattened by a Suburban.

"Those horseless carriages are much faster than my horses."

And like that, he broke the tense moment, making her laugh, because instead of looking shaken at almost ending up like a crepe, he looked terribly intrigued as he stared after the vehicle as it sped away, school stickers plastered across the back windshield, window down, pop music blaring out, and a cigarette hanging out the window.

"All the buildings have so many windows. Do they not fear attack?"

"No, unless it's hurricane season, and then everyone boards up the windows."

He watched as a couple came outside and the man held the door, and as Penelope reached out, he reached around and opened the door for her with a slight bow.

"After you, my lady."

"Thank you, kind sir." She was a grown woman, thirty-nine years old, and yet she felt like a giddy high school girl again being around Thomas, having fun bantering with him. The man had a quick wit and an easy laugh, traits she loved.

They were seated in a booth next to the window so he could look outside, and she'd given him the seat facing the door so he could watch the people in the restaurant. The place was cozy, from the traditional red and white checkered tablecloths to the painting of dogs playing poker on the wall. It was set up to offer sit-down dining and also offered carry-out, a good choice based on Thomas's reaction to all the people on vacation taking time out from the beach to grab a bite to eat.

In the short time they'd spent together, she had decided he was either suffering from a delusion or...well, the alternative might make her head explode. Where was he from? The waitress approached, pen poised above her pad.

"What can I get y'all to drink?"

"Going full octane today. Pepsi for me."

Thomas looked around and pointed to the couple seated at table next to them.

"Ale."

"Light or regular beer?"

He looked perplexed, so Penelope spoke up. "Regular."

Seeing the look on his face, she explained. "She wanted to know if you wanted a light beer, one that has less alcohol, or the full amount. I figured you would want the full amount."

"Ale is not heavy. Are the men here so weak they cannot hold a cup of ale?" He sneered at the man seated diagonally from them who was drinking a glass of water. "What is a calorie?"

"Something that strikes fear into the hearts of woman everywhere."

The change was instant: Thomas scanned the room, hand twitching next to his hip, so alert that he almost vibrated, seeking any danger around them, making her feel as if he'd stand and hold off an entire army of calories wishing to do damage to her waistline. It was a primal reaction, one that made the base woman inside her sit up and take notice. This was a man who would always put her first, defend her with his own body if necessary, and love her until the end of time. Either he was an incredibly gifted actor suffering from the belief he was a medieval knight, or he *was* a medieval knight... Right now she didn't care. She could talk to him for hours and feel like mere moments had passed, so she'd enjoy their time together and give thanks they had found each other. Whatever was wrong with him, she'd help him face it head-on.

"No, they're not something you can see. Calories are in

food, nothing really bad. When people eat too many of them, they gain weight. I'll explain more later. You said you were from England?"

He nodded at her, his posture relaxing as he examined the fork and the knife, touching the tines of the fork and testing the blade of the knife. When he ran his finger across it, he made a face of distaste before putting it down.

"It isn't very sharp. How will we cut our meat?"

"The knife is sharp enough for the pizza, or you can hold it in your hands, like those people." She pointed across the restaurant. "You're going to love pizza."

The waitress brought their drinks and, realizing he was at a loss for what to order, Penelope took charge.

"A large pizza with all the meats and extra cheese, pan style."

He took a sip of the ale and frowned. "This does not taste like proper ale."

"No? I guess the beers are more full-bodied in England?" She studied him as he drank, looking like he fit in, except he was much better looking than anyone around, and his bearing marked him as some type of aristocrat. But the more she studied him, and watched him studying not only the people coming and going and how they were dressed, but how they used their fork and knife to eat, she couldn't help herself. The signs were all there, laid out for her. Why didn't she believe?

"What's the date?"

He looked at her. "Lady?"

"The last day that you remember, what was the date? You know, the year?"

He leaned back in the chair, taking up all the room in the café, his presence filling the space around them, blotting everyone else out.

"Aye, I remember the date well—'twas the day my home burned to the ground."

"That's terrible. What happened?"

Very matter-of-fact, he told her about Oakwick Manor catching fire, how it was thought a candle tipped over, but he wasn't sure after a mysterious man was seen leaving the estate. His brother and sister, along with the stables and horses, were saved. He'd begun to tell her about his ventures as a wool merchant when the waitress brought their pizza. Thomas leaned so close to the pie that she thought he might burn his nose.

"The smell—I fear I am drooling. This is the pizza you spoke of?"

"You think it smells divine, wait until you taste it."

She took a slice and put it on his plate, and another on her own plate.

"Once it cools down, you can pick it up and eat it like them." She gestured to the couple next to them. "Or if you want to go ahead and dig in now, you can eat it like this."

She picked up her fork and knife and showed him how to cut it, since he acted like he'd never seen a fork before.

Thomas took a bite, closing his eyes, the look on his face making Penelope look around.

"'Tis even better than it smells." He opened his eyes, took another huge bite, and chewed, the look of pure bliss on his face telling her she'd picked the right place to eat.

"This food is delicious. Might we have more?"

Penelope laughed and waved over the waitress to order a second large pizza.

She waited until he'd eaten the second slice and helped himself to another before she reminded him of his story.

"Your lovely home burned down and you were about to tell me the date."

"August. The Year of Our Lord 1305."

Penelope's fork clattered against the plate. "1305? As in more than six hundred years ago?"

He looked at her, looked around the restaurant, out the window at the cars. In a quiet voice, he said, "What year is it, lady?"

"1999."

"How is it possible?" He wiped his mouth on the paper napkin and finished off the rest of his beer. Seeing the distress he was in, Penelope caught the waitress as she went by and ordered another, along with a glass of wine for her. She had a feeling she was going to need it.

"I was abducted, taken to the cliffs, where Roger and his men meant to kill me. There was a terrible storm—the earth trembled under our feet and gave way as we went over the cliff, fell to the sea. When I surfaced, there was no sign of Roger." He ate another slice of pizza, chewing thoughtfully as she picked up her slice to finish it but put it back down, her stomach protesting. By the time their drinks arrived, he had composed himself.

"A sea monster pulled me under, and when I woke, 'twas to your face on the beach."

She sipped the wine, thinking. "The wounds? Did you get them fighting Roger and his men?"

"Aye."

Penelope couldn't quite believe it. "Nature is powerful. Here it was the summer solstice, a day of great power and blood. Somehow you traveled through time." She took another sip of the wine. "Though I wouldn't have believed it if I hadn't found you myself."

The part of her in tune with nature believed his story, but the rational mind wasn't so eager to get on board. It said, *Hold on, he just took a blow to the head and is suffering some kind of brain trauma. Take him to a doctor.* But...had she and her friends somehow conjured him here? Was this all her fault because she'd wished for him? If it was, how could she ever forgive herself for stealing him from his life?

He looked longingly at the empty plate in front of them, making her laugh.

"Don't worry, we'll get pizza again. Wait until you have dessert."

As they left, instead of going back to the car, he offered her his arm, and they walked along the path that meandered around the shopping center. There were several fountains, and with the nice weather, kids were playing on the grassy areas while tired parents looked on. The smell of freshly cut grass made her inhale deeply, and she caught the scent of him again.

Thomas didn't say much. He was too busy looking at everything, his eyes lingering on the women.

"They aren't wearing any clothes!"

"Of course they are. They have on shorts and tank tops, like you've seen me wear. That woman is wearing a sundress, and that one, well, her skirt is short enough to qualify for not wearing anything. You think this is scandalous, wait until we get home and the beach bathers are out. A bikini is going to knock you on your ass."

He grinned for the first time. "I think mayhap I will like this bikini you speak of. Might you wear one?"

"If you're sweet, I might." She swatted him playfully. "You're a red-blooded male; of course you'll like bikinis." She laughed. "Come on, let me introduce you to a cupcake."

Chapter Nine

Full from pizza and dessert, Penelope was in a stupor as she drove home, though Thomas, who had eaten almost two pizzas and four cupcakes, was fascinated by the workings of the car after overcoming his fear of the "metal beast," as he called it. He asked about everything, from the motor to the tires to the buttons, which he kept pushing, rolling the windows up and down, and for the first time since she'd gotten the MG, she wished she'd gotten the car with electric windows—he would've had fun making them go up and down —but her car was totally old school.

There was a new song by Ricky Martin, "Livin' la Vida Loca," that was really catchy, and she turned up the radio, singing along softly. Thomas tapped his fingers against his thigh as they drove back across the bridge to her house, and when she pulled in the driveway, parking under the carport, he stopped her. "Can we hear the end? This tune is pleasing to my ears."

"Of course we can wait. It's a really catchy tune. Let me put the top up while we listen."

He helped her, and then, stroking the dash as he would a horse, turned in the seat to face her.

"Mistress Penelope? Might I try driving your horseless carriage?"

"It would be easier if it were an automatic, mine's a manual, but...I think we can drive over to the farmers' market lot. It's big and empty, nothing to hit. I'll give you a lesson."

"I cannot wait." He rubbed his hands together, and she wondered if she were creating a monster—the more time they spent together, the more she was attracted to him and was starting to accept he was telling the truth, and somehow, someway, the universe had sent a man across time...for her.

After taking the keys from her, he expertly inserted them into the lock, opened the door, and stood back, letting her go in first. She could certainly get used to a man like this.

"Would you like a glass of wine?"

"I will pour. I've developed quite a fondness for the wine you call Frog's Leap." He rubbed his belly. "Do you think we might have another cupcake?"

She laughed, thinking of him eating all those cupcakes after dinner, and wondering where he put them.

"Of course. Why do you think I brought three home? But I'll do you one better: I'll show you how to make them."

The evening deepened to night, and Thomas was yawning when she stood. "I made up the guest room for you."

He followed her into the cheery room, and she watched

him gently sit down on the bed, testing it out.

"'Tis so soft and the cloth so fine." He turned the lamp on the nightstand on and off several times, completely intrigued, and she made a mental note to show him how to search the internet in the morning.

"Goodnight, Thomas."

"Sleep well...Penelope."

She pulled the door shut behind her with a goofy smile on her face, and went to get ready for bed.

The next morning, she showered and braided her hair down her back then went out looking for Thomas, only to find him on the deck, his mouth hanging open as he looked at the people on the beach. They'd both overslept, and it was already close to ten, the beach filling up with weekend visitors.

"Do you see what they're wearing? The women are practically naked." He turned to her, an astonished look on his face, and she couldn't help it: she tried to keep it in, but she busted out laughing.

"I was wondering when you'd notice the women in bikinis. I know it's a lot of skin, but it's nothing unusual. It's how women go to the beach today."

He turned and looked at her, his gaze traveling from her head to her toes, making her insides liquefy.

"Where is your garment?"

Penelope's cheeks heated up, and, very much unlike her, she felt shy.

"Under my dress. Some of my friends say I'm getting a little bit old to rock a bikini, but I've always figured you should wear what you're comfortable in."

"Might we go for a walk on the beach while you wear this bikini?"

"We did buy a swimsuit for you yesterday, so I'm sure we can do that, but let's have breakfast first, start the day out right."

He followed her inside, stopping to wipe his feet on the mat so he wouldn't track sand into the house, then he immediately went over and turned on the music. She had speakers throughout the house, and the sounds of Vivaldi filled the air.

"I thought we'd have a big breakfast. Being out in the water and the sun always makes me hungry. Do you like waffles, bacon, and eggs?"

"What are waffles?"

"You know how you like cupcakes? You're going to love waffles." She tied on an retro-style apron so she wouldn't get her sundress messy, and rummaged in the cabinets, pulling out the griddle and supplies to make the waffles. She always added a touch of amaretto and fresh blueberries to hers. While she got out the rest of the dishes, he took them and set the table without her asking.

"Did you ever set your own table at home?"

He looked up, in the process of placing floral cloth napkins next to the Vietri china. "Nay, the servants would do this, but I find I like working beside you."

After he'd set the table, he came over and looked interested, so she put him to work.

"Why don't you measure the ingredients for the waffles? Here's the recipe. Let me know if you have any questions and I'll get started on the bacon and eggs. How do you like your eggs?"

"Cooked."

She grinned at him. "I think I'll make us both scrambled today, and tomorrow I'll introduce you to quiche." The way he'd eaten so far, she cooked him six eggs and twelve pieces of bacon, and decided if he was still hungry she could always cook more. Where did he put it? The guy didn't have an ounce of fat on him. If she ate like that, she'd blow up like a balloon.

It had been a long time since Penelope cooked next to a man in the kitchen—her last husband deemed it women's work and refused to lift a finger—but she'd always thought a man who would cook for you or with you was a good man to hold on to. And while she'd really thought she'd never get married again—after all, eight times was a lot for anyone—she felt the familiar stirrings of interest as they worked companionably together, though this time was different, easier, and they fit together as if they'd been a couple for at least a decade, one of those annoying couples still madly in love after ten or twenty years, genuinely fascinated and interested in the other person.

As they sat down to eat, Penelope couldn't believe the mound of food set out for two people, but the look on Thomas's face made it all worthwhile.

"Dig in."

He took a bite of the crispy bacon, and the look of ecstasy on his face made her want to laugh.

"Saints, this is delicious." He ate another piece of bacon before trying the eggs, with similar results.

"Wait until you try the blueberry waffles. Put a little bit of butter and maple syrup on them."

He did as she suggested, and as Penelope chewed, she watched his face.

"Can we have these again?"

"Of course."

"For breakfast every day? 'Tis a good way to break one's fast."

"Perhaps not every day. These are more of a weekend thing. If I ate like this every day, I'd get fat."

He stopped mid-chew and swallowed, looking her over. "You are not fat. You have a body that makes a man want to take hold of you and keep you in his bed for a fortnight at least."

She ducked her head, surprised at the shyness that bubbled up, and took a sip of her champagne. On the weekend she loved to have champagne or a Bloody Mary for brunch.

It was so nice, sitting together on the weekend, having the whole day to spend with someone. Such a simple act, preparing and eating a meal together, yet it filled her heart, and she felt more content than she had in a long time.

When they were finished, Thomas helped her clear the table. She opened the dishwasher to put the dishes in, and he looked at her.

"It's called a dishwasher. None of this is coming back to you?"

"We have no such thing in my time."

"You rinse and I'll load."

He rinsed off the dishes, taking his time, and it was evident it was the first time he'd ever done it.

She loaded up the dishwasher and got the soap out, and when she turned it on, he jumped.

"You'll get used to the sound. It's actually pretty quiet."

With a look outside at the beautiful blue sky, Penelope pointed to the ocean. "Want to change into your swimsuit and spend the day outside?"

"I cannot wait to see this bikini."

And with that, she ran for the sunscreen and beach towels.

Chapter Ten

Between Thomas looking at all the people and remarking on the lack of proper clothing, Penelope was ready for an afternoon cocktail. It had been a perfect day: they swam in the ocean, walked on the sand, and spent time talking to each other, learning more about each other's lives. She had a deep respect for his sense of honor and duty, and the niggling worry that somehow she was responsible for his being here made her feel awful inside.

And while it had taken her a while to come to terms with his story, she had finally accepted he wasn't suffering some kind of head trauma and indeed had been transported from medieval England to North Carolina. Why here and not modern-day England? Tomorrow she'd sit down with Rainbow and get her take on the whole situation.

By four, they'd gotten enough sun. Thomas carried their towels, and both walked fast across the sand, though it was always the hottest in the strip right before the walkway.

"Yikes, the sand is hotter than Hades today—"

She was cut off as she found herself swept up in his arms.

"You were saying?"

That amazing man carried her the rest of the way to the house, putting her down next to the outdoor shower so they could both rinse off.

"I could get used to being carried across the sand. You'll spoil me."

"A woman is to be cherished. I would carry you to the ends of the earth to hear the lilt of your voice, see your smile, and hear your laughter."

And what did she say to that? He was perfect, and yet she could not keep him no matter how much she had begun to want to. He belonged to another time, had a life, responsibilities...but if he couldn't get back? Then maybe they might have a future together.

"I have not spent a day doing nothing since I was a small lad. I thank you, Penelope."

"Sometimes doing nothing is the best thing of all," she said as she opened the door and they went inside to shower. As she washed out her bikini, Penelope smelled the ocean, the sun, and the suntan lotion. The combination of smells was her favorite.

She had to admit, she was enjoying spending time with Thomas. By the time she'd finished showering, getting dressed and putting lotion on her body, he was sprawled on the sofa looking like he belonged, and had already poured them each a glass of wine.

"You look beautiful today. The pink dress reminds me of

roses." He stood up as she approached, waiting until she sat before he sat back down.

"Thank you. I thought I'd show you how to search the internet. That way you can look up electricity, cars, and... search for your family, find out what happened to them. But Thomas?"

He looked up, the hope on his face enough to make her heart still for a moment.

"Aye?"

"Unless they did something historically important, there might not be any information. I just don't want you to get your hopes up."

He pointed to the laptop on the table. "Truly? I can learn all this information from this tiny box?"

"You can. Let me show you." And she spent the next half-hour showing him how to search, crossing her fingers he'd find something.

She left him to his own devices while she went upstairs to the attic that had been renovated into a small home office. Penelope was fortunate—she worked from home writing copy for various companies, something that wouldn't have been possible before the internet. Engrossed in her work, she spent the next several hours catching up. Didn't matter it was the weekend; she always had work to do, and she wanted to get ahead, knowing she would be spending more time with Thomas.

When she came back downstairs, he was pale. "Thomas? What's wrong?"

He didn't say anything, pointing to the screen instead, and as she stepped closer to look, she could see a beautiful home.

"Is that your home?"

He nodded, tried to speak, and had to clear his throat. Penelope went to the kitchen and got him a glass of water, and then, on second thought, poured him another glass of wine.

"Here, this will help."

He drank deeply before meeting her eyes.

"Oakwick Manor does still stand, but I can find no mention of what happened to Josephine and Heath. Is there anywhere else we might look?"

Her heart ached at seeing the anguish on his face. "We can go into town—there's a used bookstore, and they always have a decent-size history section. We can also go to the library, but they're closed until Monday."

He was lucky; he'd only found mention of his home because some student had done a paper at a big university and it was online.

The TV might help to distract him. Up to now she'd avoided the television, rarely watching it herself, but when she turned it on, he jumped up from the sofa and walked over to the screen, touching the people moving around.

"Hello? You there, tiny human?"

She resisted laughing. Barely. "They can't hear you. It's like a play, but they show it in people's homes. That's the best way I know to describe television."

It was funny—when she handed him the remote after showing him how to work it, he quickly took charge, flipping through the channels, stopping here and there, and then she heard him exclaim and saw he'd stopped on a channel with a

British guy talking about Scotland and England.

"As much as I want you to find out what happened, are you sure it's a good idea? You're going to find out things, and if you can go back, you might change history."

He tore his attention from the screen to stare at her thoughtfully, looking sad.

"I do not believe I can go back. I do not know why, only that I feel it as certain as I know the sun will shine tomorrow."

"Then watch away. I need to run to the grocery—do you mind if I leave you here?" She knew if she took him it would take five times as long; he'd be fascinated by everything in the store, and while she was happy to let him look at everything, she wanted to get in and out today. She had a cake to make for Rainbow—it was her birthday, and they always celebrated at midnight.

"Nay, Penelope, I will enjoy watching the little people on the glass."

And didn't he sound just like an aristocrat as he basically dismissed her? She knew he didn't mean anything by it, and it made her chuckle to herself as she grabbed her keys and left him stretched out on the sofa, a glass of wine in one hand, the remote in the other. Maybe she would get her happy ending after all.

Chapter Eleven

At the end of the "program" about the homes still standing in his country, the man talking showed a home that made Thomas leap off the sofa. 'Twas *his* home. It still stood so many years later. He traced the towers, looking for any sign to tell him what happened to those he cared for.

The man pointed to the towers, one at the front of the house and the other in the courtyard at the rear, and said they both remained to this day and were owned by the DeChartes family.

"Roger. Whoreson." Thomas spat as he recoiled from the screen. How had Roger taken his home? And what had happened to Josephine and Heath? As words appeared on the screen, Thomas heard the man say the family who owned it before were wealthy wool merchants—the eldest son fought as a mercenary and amassed quite a bit of gold winning tourneys. And that was it; the man said nothing more, and the show ended. No matter how long Thomas waited, there was nothing more about his home. When Penelope returned from her hunting and gathering, he would speak to her see if there was anything else they could find out about his family and how Roger had managed to steal his home.

That night, Thomas was asleep when a sound woke him, and before he knew it he had rolled out of the bed, crouched on the floor, his hands searching for his missing sword. Had someone broken into the house? Padding across the floor, he paused at the door and listened. There were sounds coming from the kitchen, so he picked up a heavy candlestick from the table and made his way to the kitchen. On the way, he stopped at her room, saw the door ajar, and pushed it open, the candlestick raised. His stomach clenched at the empty bed. He would destroy every single ruffian who dared touch her golden skin.

Thomas burst into the kitchen, candlestick brandished over his head, and slid to a stop. Penelope had her baking instruments scattered across what she called an island.

"Oh, sorry, I was trying to be quiet. Did I wake you?" She peered at him, a spot of flour on her cheek. "Why do you have a candlestick? The lights work fine. Remember the switches?"

Slowly, the battle rage left his body, and he lowered the candlestick, sheepishly placing it on the counter.

"I woke and heard noises, thought men with ill intent had broken into your home and were stealing you away."

She blinked at him before smiling. "It was very nice of you to come to my rescue."

He stood up straight. "Of course I would rescue you, my lady. What kind of man would cower like a dog while his lady faced danger?" Then he tilted his head up, sniffing. "Do I smell cupcakes?"

"I'm baking a cake for my friend Rainbow. Want to help?"

He peered out the windows into a blackness so dark that he couldn't even see the ocean, though he could hear it, then he looked back at her, mouth agape.

"'Tis the middle of the night."

"It is. Ever since I was little, my eccentric grandmother, Lucy Lou Merriweather, would wake my sisters and I up at midnight on our birthdays. We would traipse down to the kitchen, where we would have cake. Each of us liked a different kind. I'm like my nieces; I love angel food cake with cream cheese frosting. But Rainbow, Rainbow loves chocolate cake with chocolate icing, so that's what I'm making."

"Rainbow is a strange name." He took a step closer, the scents making his mouth water, and as he approached, she went still, her feminine smell permeating the air. He reached out his thumb, wiping the spot of flour from her cheek. Her skin was so soft, and up close she smelled like roses and the sun and of her baking smells.

"You had flour on your cheek." The moment stretched

between them. Thomas wanted to pull her to him, nibble her lips, and tell her all the things he had imagined, but he stepped back. Until he knew without a doubt he could not go back, help his siblings, and save Oakwick, he could not make her his, no matter how much he wished it otherwise.

"You smell like roses."

"Do I?" She put a hand to her cheek, running a finger across her lip. He tracked her movements, wanting to remove her finger and replace it with his lips.

"I make a cream for my face. This batch has rose petals in it." Her hand trembled, and it pleased him to see she was as affected by him as he was by her. Since he had arrived, he'd been drawn to this bewitching woman, felt the pull of her even when she wasn't close to him. 'Twas almost like a fever, one he would gladly endure forever to make her his. Blasted responsibilities.

He touched her cheek again. "Aye, your skin is as soft as a rose." Then he smelled something delicious, but it looked rather like mud.

"I'm getting ready to pour the batter in the pan. Want to lick the spoon?"

The brown paste did not look appetizing, but when she finished scraping it into a pan and put it in the oven to bake, she turned to him and handed him the bowl and the spoon.

"Have at it. But eat it in the kitchen so you don't get chocolate on the sofa."

The first bite was hard to describe, as if heaven had exploded in his mouth. The second, he tasted a hint of raspberries, and the third, he put the spoon in the sink and used his finger to get every drop of the delightful stuff.

Penelope efficiently cleaned up the kitchen, removed her apron, and for a moment he forgot about the precious batter. She was dressed in a short purple gown with no sleeves that shimmered in the light, and he could see her shapely legs and arms.

"You are so beautiful."

She turned a fetching shade of the palest pink. "Thank you. I always wear an apron when I cook. Didn't want to get any batter on my nightgown. It looked like you enjoyed the cake batter."

He peered sadly into the empty bowl then up at her. "Is there any more?"

"Wait until you try the icing." She grinned, and he washed the bowl, then put it in the dishwasher, as he had seen her do before.

"Will it be long to make this icing?" he asked hopefully, eyeing the bowl on the counter.

Penelope hung her apron over the chair. "I'm going to sit outside and listen to the waves for a few minutes while I call Rainbow and find out when she'll be home. She keeps erratic hours, and I want to make sure she's there—in this heat, the icing will melt. When I come back in, I'll get the dishwasher going and make the icing. You can help, if you'd like."

"Make haste, woman."

With that, she laughed, making him wish again he had no other responsibilities and could stay in this strange land with her for all time, grow old with her, sitting together, holding hands and watching the sun set over the water.

Chapter Twelve

Penelope was outside, leaning over the rail, looking at the moonlight rippling across the waves as she talked to her friend. Thomas had never met anyone like her before. She made him laugh and wish he could take her back with him, but he knew she would not wish to leave the marvels of her time, and she would stand out as too different. People would think she was cursed, and he'd spend his life protecting her, but he feared it would not be enough, and one day an overzealous priest would take her away to be burned.

Wanting to aid her, Thomas decided he could turn on the machine that washed the dishes. A marvel that he itched to take apart and find out how it worked. The time it would save in his home. The soap was located under the sink, and he'd watched her pour it into the little cup in the machine to feed it.

He poured a bit in and frowned. It didn't look like enough

to clean so many dishes, so he added more until it was full. Then he saw another cup beside the first one, so he poured the soap in there as well. And finally, he'd seen her add something blue—she said it made the dishes shine, and while he didn't think it mattered if they were shiny as long as they were clean, he looked for the blue liquid.

The bottle he found was bigger than the one she'd used. It said *liquid dish soap* on the front, and was for washing dishes. Where did the blue stuff go? Thomas looked for another cup but didn't see one. Shrugging, he squirted it into the machine until it covered the shallow, big pan, and shut it quick so it would not run on the floor. Satisfied, he pushed the button to wake the machine. Pleased he had aided her in her tasks, Thomas looked outside to see her sitting on the sofa in the screened-in porch, where she said the mesh protected her from bugs. The sound of her laughter came through the door, and he smiled, watching her for several minutes as she spoke to her friend, content to see the emotions play across her face. But he wished he was holding her against him.

The machine made noises, a bit louder than before, but it sounded quite hungry, so Thomas went to take a shower. He knew he would sleep no more this night.

The shriek came as he was drying off, quickly wrapping the towel around his waist, and he swore, feeling the loss of his blades, and ran to the kitchen, sliding across water, almost losing his balance.

"What has happened?"

Penelope stopped the dishwasher, ankle deep in suds, and turned to see him looking helplessly at the still-overflowing dishwasher and floor. But she did not yell; instead, she summoned up patience from a deep reserve and took a deep breath.

"Thomas, what did you put in the dishwasher?"

He gaped at the avalanche of soapsuds filling up the kitchen, so she tried again.

"Thomas. Focus. What kind of soap did you use? Show me."

Shaking his head, he met her gaze. "I only wanted to aid you, as you have no servants. I filled both cups with the stuff from the box under the sink, but I could not find the small bottle of blue liquid to make the dishes shine. I found a much larger bottle instead."

"Oh no. The little blue bottle was empty, and you only add it to the dishwasher every few months. Please tell me you didn't use the liquid dish soap?"

He nodded, reaching down to touch the bubbles, rubbing them between his fingers before smelling a bubble and sneezing.

"Aye. The pan is much larger than the small cup, but 'tis shallow, so I filled it."

For a moment she could only blink at him. "You mean the door of the dishwasher?"

He blinked. "Aye, I shut it fast so none would leak out..." Though he trailed off, realizing the silliness of the statement, she guessed.

"No wonder." The tickle started in her belly and traveled up her throat and nose as she wheezed. "Oh my, that's what happened. The liquid dish soap is for washing the dishes by hand. It never goes in the dishwasher, or..." She busted out laughing, bent over, hands on her knees, tears falling. "...this is what happens." She gestured around the kitchen, laughing so hard that her stomach hurt.

A fluffy towel was thrust into her hands.

"I am truly sorry. I only wished to aid you. You have no servants."

Penelope looked up into his kind face. "It's okay, it was a mistake. But we're going to need more towels."

"I will fetch them."

"Fetch them all, every one you can find," she called out after him.

While he did, she opened the dishwasher and took out the dishes, stacking them in the sink, then pulled out every dish towel and cloth napkin she owned and blotted up the soap suds, giggles escaping as she worked.

"I have them all."

She turned in time to see Thomas—the stack of towels so high that he couldn't see—slip in the suds. The towels went up in the air, his arms windmilling to regain his balance, and she lunged to catch the towels. They collided, falling together, and he somehow rolled and used his body to cushion her fall so she landed on top of him.

And then, well, she was at a total loss for words, as his

hands were in her hair and he pulled her down, trailing kisses across her shoulder and throat, shifting so every inch of her was pressed against him.

"I've been thinking about kissing you since I opened my eyes to see you on the beach."

"Me too." He captured her mouth, pressing his lips to hers, tasting of chocolate and smelling of soap and male, and that faint scent of leather and steel that always surrounded him. There on the kitchen floor, enveloped in soapsuds, Penelope lost herself in Thomas as the kiss went on and on. He tasted every part of her mouth, making her groan.

Unable to form words, she ran her hands through his hair, kissing him deeply, lost in the man. The voice calling out made her jump, hitting her head on the chair. How had they ended up halfway under the kitchen table?

"Hello? Pittypat. It's me, Mildred."

With a sigh, they broke apart, the towel around Thomas's hips soaked from the soap, as was her dress. They looked like they'd been caught in a rainstorm and hadn't cared, so caught up in each other that everything else faded away.

She touched his bicep. "Go, get dressed."

"One more." He pulled her close, crushing her to him, and with one more toe-curling kiss, he stalked to the bedroom, leaving her standing in soap suds, looking like a drowned rat, one finger tracing her lips. That was how Mildred found Penelope when she let herself in at two in the morning.

"What on earth?"

Penelope laughed again. "What on earth is right. What are you doing up at two a.m.?"

Her sister frowned at the mess. "There's a bulletin out for an escaped convict, and he looks like your homeless man." She thrust a piece of paper at Penelope.

Taking the paper, she skimmed it. "No, Thomas doesn't have any tattoos. It isn't him. Couldn't this have waited until morning?"

Mildred sniffed. "No. You know I do worry about you, sister. You can't be too careful nowadays."

They talked for a few more minutes, Mildred offering to help clean up the mess, but Penelope wanted her to go home. The moment between her and Thomas had been shattered, leaving her annoyed.

"Thank you for your concern. Now go home and get some sleep so I can clean up this mess and finish Rainbow's cake."

Chapter Thirteen

"How will I ever repay you for all you have done for me?" Thomas admired his form in the looking glass. He was brown from the sun, his hair the color it was when he was a child, and for the first time in many years, the worry and strain of caring for his people and family no longer weighed heavily upon his shoulders. Being with her, he had laughed and smiled more than he had in...he could not remember. Mayhap when he was a child.

Penelope and her friends had tried many rituals over several fortnights to send him back, but alas, none had borne fruit, and while they were discouraged, he accepted that the fates wished him to be in this new land with a woman he could not imagine how he had ever lived without. Every morning he woke, desperate to hear the sound of her voice, the soft lilt, and to see the smile she always had ready for him, as if he were the most important person in her entire world. It made him stand tall, wish to be the man he saw in her eyes.

'Twas an odd feeling to have someone take care of him, when all his life he had taken care of others with no thought to his own welfare. She made a living writing for companies, and he was amazed how she could come up with such descriptions that made him able to see the product she was working on. In truth, he would slay a thousand men on the field of battle to make his way home to her, just to hear her laugh, to see her smile, and to feel the touch of her lips against his.

"Repay me? Why? If our situations were reversed and I had ended up in medieval England, you would have done the same for me." Then she laughed. "No, you would have branded me a witch and I'd be nothing more than a crispy piece of bacon."

"Aye. Mayhap you are right—my servants would say you bewitched me, and in truth, I believe you have, though I would gladly be bewitched by you for all eternity."

"Oh, my." Penelope fanned herself, and he grinned, pleased she favored him.

"Shall we go?" she said as she opened the door. "You're going to love seeing the fireworks from the water."

"Penelope?"

"Yes?" She turned to look at him, her shorts showing off her long, tan legs, her high shoes making him think about her curves as he pulled her close and knelt, first to kiss each toe, the blue of a daytime sky. He trailed kisses up her leg and knee, and then she pulled him to his feet and touched his face. Her soft lips brushed his chin, the scar on his cheek, and then his lips. She sighed into his mouth, and he lifted her, pulling her close, wanting to never let go.

Her phone sliced through the moment, and she tilted her head back, a dazed look on her face, her lips red and swollen, her hair in disarray.

"Dratted phone."

The annoyance in her voice made him chuckle as she looked at the number and ignored the call.

"Might you need these?" He held her keys and tiny purse out to her, a grin spreading across his face. He had made her this flustered with his compliments and kisses.

The pink bloomed across her chest, moving up her neck like the sun coming up over the water in the morning. He had never been so content as he touched each freckle across her nose and cheeks, connecting the dots to match the stars in the night sky.

"Right. I knew you had them." She turned a brighter shade of pink as he locked the door behind them.

Without a word, she let him open the passenger door for her. She'd said he needed a card to drive, but when he'd questioned her on how to get one, she'd thought and laughed, saying she gave money to the police, and so she thought they'd be okay as long as he didn't do anything crazy. With no birth certificate or other ID, it would be difficult to procure proper documents for him, but her friend Rainbow knew someone who might be able to aid him.

Thomas settled into the small car and put the top down as she tied a scarf on her head to protect her hair from the wind. He loved her hair flowing down her back and blown about by the breeze, as if the very air wanted to caress the locks as much as he did. With her sunglasses firmly in place, he put his own on—Aviator sunglasses, she'd called them—and started up the engine.

"Listen how she purrs for me."

"You're involved in quite the love affair with my car."

He patted the steering wheel. "Do not listen to her, my love. She would not understand."

Penelope rolled her eyes. "I don't know what it is with men and cars, but you have a gift. She hasn't run this well in years."

"She likes me." Thomas had spent time at a garage across the bridge and learned how the metal beasts worked. 'Twas fascinating, and he'd spent hours working on the beautiful red car until she purred and went faster than Penelope said she ever had.

He shifted the gears and drove them to the marina, where she said they were taking a boat out on the water to watch the fireworks. Explosions of color. He could not wait to see such marvels. Her country was so young, and he liked they celebrated its birth.

"You know I have the same birthday as your country."

"Wait. What?" She looked over her sunglasses at him. "July fourth? Today is your birthday? Oh, Thomas, you should have told me. We would have celebrated this morning."

He chuckled. "Your blueberry waffles are celebration enough. We will mark the occasion by watching the colors in the sky tonight." Her palm was warm as he twined their fingers together, admiring the shape of her fingers. Would he ever stop noticing new things about her? On her littlest finger were three freckles, and he raised her hand to his lips, kissing each one.

"You've tried lots of kinds of cake. Do you have a favorite yet?" She was looking out the window, watching a hawk circle lazily in the afternoon sky.

"Aye, the chocolate cake with the chocolate and raspberry icing. It is powerful good." He looked hopefully into the small area behind them at the basket. "Might there be cake tonight?"

Late that night, Thomas drove them home, marveling at the fireworks that exploded across the night sky in so many colors and shapes. His favorite had been the dragon. It was green and breathed red fire. 'Twas the best day of his birth he could remember. When he turned off the engine, he looked over to see Penelope had fallen asleep, so he lifted her out. He'd come back down and put the top up after he carried her inside.

She didn't wake as he carried her up the stairs and put her in the bed, removing the pretty blue shoes and covering her. As he turned, she reached out, mumbling.

"Stay, just for a minute. Don't leave me."

"As if I could survive a day without your smile, love." He stretched out on top of the blankets and gathered her close, stroking her hair, working out each tangle.

"Penelope, I know you are sad you could not find a way to send me home, but...I am pleased. I wish to make a life with you, and will spend every day worshipping you. I love you with all my heart."

He looked over to find she was asleep and had not heard him. His family ring winked in the light from the hall, and he decided he would ask one of her friends where he could find a goldsmith to fashion her a proper ring, for he meant to marry her and make her his. Thomas had waited his entire life to find her, and he would never let her go. With a kiss on her forehead, he got up and went down to put the top up on the car.

Chapter Fourteen

"How long has Thomas been here? It seems like he's always been a part of your life." Rainbow waggled her eyebrows at Penelope as they stretched out on turquoise chaise lounges next to the pool and sipped sweet tea with mint. The endless summer days made her wish the warmth would never turn to fall and then to a time of renewal in winter, but Penelope knew change was the one constant in life, and she had to embrace it or risk becoming one of those people who ended up adrift in life, never growing or moving forward, stagnant and trapped in the web of life.

"Mildred was complaining yesterday she hadn't heard from me in weeks. Honestly, I hadn't noticed how fast time had passed. It's so much fun seeing Thomas experience the little things in life we take for granted. He spent hours at the marina last week talking to the fisherman about everything from rope to the ship's engines. The zest and excitement he has for life is so refreshing."

The man in question was currently shirtless, tan and breathtaking as he gleefully knocked down the last of the rickety wooden fence surrounding the pool. The replacement fence, black iron with decorative finials, gleamed in the sunlight.

"So let's see: it was the day after the summer solstice, so he's been with me a little over two months. Can you believe tomorrow is the first of September? And as hard as it is to accept, I believe he was sent through time for a reason—for what, I have no idea. I'm just happy he's here with me."

Rainbow had always possessed a special sense, and was able to predict events. Many in town scoffed, but there were others who were afraid of her, believing she indeed had some kind of mystical powers, and on days like today, as the spoon in Rainbow's iced tea kept lazily stirring without any aid from her, Penelope was inclined to agree.

Inquisitive golden cat eyes turned her way. "He's here for you."

Penelope almost choked on her tea. "Wait, you're just going to leave me hanging?" She studied Thomas as he worked, the muscles rippling across skin. He looked happy enough, but not knowing what happened to his family, now long dead...it had to be a terrible burden on anyone, let alone a man who lived and breathed words like, honor, duty, and responsibility.

She'd told him she'd hire someone to put up the new fence, but he said he enjoyed physical labor, and without his sword and opponents to fight against, he didn't want to run to fat. As if. The man would give the Man of Steel a run for his money any day.

"Thomas is fated for you." Rainbow looked troubled as she ran a hand through pale blue hair. "But sweetie...you're not going to grow old together. I don't know what's going to happen; wish I did. I only know your time together is special, and you both have to wring every second of joy out of life while you have each other."

Penelope turned to look at Rainbow, horror threatening to drown her. "Please tell me we didn't cause this with the summer solstice celebration? He arrived the next morning. I wondered, but nothing has ever happened—well, except for that time the pelican landed on Annabelle's head and refused to leave."

"No, honey, we may have added power to whatever forces were already in play—maybe we brought him to Holden Beach—but traveling through time...no, the universe did that of its own accord."

Penelope took her best friend's hand. "Thank you for telling me. We've tried everything we could think of to send him home, and nothing worked. I guess I thought it meant he'd be here for good." Penelope watched Thomas work. "I will enjoy every second, and no matter what happens, no regrets. After all, to truly love, we have to make ourselves vulnerable, and there are no guarantees we won't end up flattened on the concrete in the end, but the fall...oh, the fall is glorious."

Rainbow laughed. "Yes, it is. The fall of love is what keeps the world from imploding." She took a drink of her tea, and the spoon went still. "Did you see there's a renaissance faire this weekend? Bet he would love going."

"That's a great idea. Maybe we can find him a sword there. Wouldn't that be a sight to see...him practicing his swordplay in the mornings on the beach while I do yoga?"

They both laughed, soaking up the sun, though Penelope kept stealing glances at Thomas, hoping he wouldn't disappear before her eyes. Then she shook her head. No, no worrying and no regrets.

Chapter Fifteen

The renaissance faire was located about an hour from Holden Beach, out in a field. It was Friday, the beginning of the holiday weekend, with Monday Labor Day, so there were still lots of vacationers at the beach, but after next week, they'd have the beach to themselves.

"Many people attend the fair?" Thomas wove in and out of traffic like he'd been doing it his whole life, and Penelope was content to be a passenger, soaking up the sun as they turned onto the road leading to the entrance. Cars were parked along the side of the road, but he wasn't having that.

"Nay, we will procure a place to park close to the gates. I will not have my car left on the side of the common road where someone might crash into her."

"I like how you and my car have such a deep understanding."

He laughed, patting the dash. "She is a fine machine."

Penelope had never been to a renaissance faire, and seeing it through his eyes made it entertaining, especially as he sneered at several exhibitions and told her "'twas not the way it was done."

"Come one, come all, we have one spot in the joust for a lucky ticket holder. Now check your numbers, ladies and gentlemen…ready? The winner is number 25421. Make your way to the red and gold tent to compete." The announcer paused. "And if you do not wish to compete, we have a lovely gift for you."

When no one came forward, Penelope pulled out their tickets and checked the numbers for the third time. "Thomas. You won."

"Truly? I can compete?"

She nodded, and he bent her backward, his mouth capturing hers, his lips firm and warm as their tongues met and danced together. When he finally let her up, she was breathless.

"Goodness."

He wore a look of supreme male satisfaction, especially when a group of college guys applauded and cheered.

"Now that I've had a proper send-off from my lady, sit and watch me win."

The arrogant tone and stride made her all giddy as she made her way to the stands, where they had a front-row seat for her, since Thomas was the lucky winner.

"Wine or champagne?" A guy dressed in green tunic and hose held out a tray.

"Bubbly would be divine. Thank you." She accepted a glass, glad they had fans going so it wasn't so stifling under the tents.

After a few matches, she was getting fidgety. When the announcer came back on, she leaned forward to get a look at Thomas, though she needn't have bothered—he stood out, making the others look like they were playing, which they were, but he looked deadly serious. She could see how he'd won so much gold in tourneys over the years. The bell sounded, and she found herself clutching the railing, wishing him success.

There were a riot of colors surrounding her, from the tents, to the costumes everyone was wearing, to the horses. Thomas wore silver and black, a great choice to match his eyes, and his horse was black and wore the same colors. His opponent was a bear of a man, dressed in green and orange, the reigning champion of the fair—not really an even match, in her opinion, but the crowd seemed to be thrilled.

Boys brought out incredibly long lances and handed them to the men, who wore silver helmets with a slit to see through. Penelope drained the bubbly, accepted another glass, and thought she would levitate out of her seat from her nerves. They galloped toward each other, the lances lowered, and in an instant, Thomas struck the man, sending him flying backward, tumbling off the horse. He landed on the ground with a thud and didn't move. The young men ran out to help the man up as he shook his head, and the crowd went wild.

Since he won, Thomas was offered the chance to fight with a sword against the current champion. She wanted to tell him to be careful, but then she thought it was his opponent who should take care, as he was fighting a living, breathing medieval man. The first sword, Thomas sneered and handed it back, and the same with the second. She laughed as she saw the resignation on his face when he accepted the third sword. The competition was over almost as fast as the joust, and Thomas split the man's shield in two, sending the guy to his knees. The crowd were on their feet, screaming.

He came to stand in front of her, and she leaned over the rail to kiss him. The cheering rose to a deafening pitch, and when she sat back, her cheeks burned. Thomas grinned.

"I needs see to my winnings."

"Go ahead, then find me at the stalls over there. I want to do a bit of shopping." She'd had the best idea for his belated birthday present. Sure, she'd taken him to dinner and made him his favorite chocolate cake with chocolate raspberry icing, but she wanted to do something special for the man she had fallen hard for. Wandering through the offerings, she spied a booth with silver glinting in the sun. There were all kinds of wicked-looking knives and daggers.

"Looking for anything in particular, my lady?"

It was odd to hear others call her "my lady"—that was what Thomas called her, and it made her smile every time to hear his accent and the affection behind the words.

"Birthday present. I was thinking two daggers."

"Excellent choice." He laid out several for her, but they weren't quite what she was looking for, and she shook her head.

The man's eyes lit up. "I have two I finished recently." He knelt and brought out two cloth-wrapped bundles, and when he pulled out the blades, she gasped.

"They're exquisite." One had flowers and vines etched along the steel, and what looked like a ruby in the hilt. The second had writing on it, and a green stone that looked like an emerald in the hilt.

"What does it say?"

He chuckled. "It's French, but it's Dr. Seuss. It says, *You know you're in love when you can't fall asleep because reality is finally better than your dreams.*"

They were outrageously expensive, but perfect for him, and she'd seen him reaching for the lost blades whenever he sensed danger.

"I'll take them. Thomas will love them. He won the joust and sword fighting today."

The man's brows went up. "Everyone's talking about him, where he studied. He is gifted."

Boy, you have no idea. "He is. Do you know where I might find him a pair of boots that he could keep the daggers in?"

This time the merchant grinned. "Like these?" He stepped out from behind the table, and she saw knee-high brown boots, which he pulled a dagger out of.

"Exactly like those."

She paid him for the daggers, and he pointed her to the merchant a few booths down for the boots. The man there was also helpful, and had boots made in Thomas's size in a soft, buttery brown leather. With her packages wrapped, she happily wandered around until she felt a hand on her arm.

"You were amazing!" She kissed him on the cheek, happy to see his eyes shining. "You're not even sweating. I saw the guy you fought with the sword. He looked like he jumped in the water with his clothes on."

"'Twas merely a bit of sport. I have talked with several men—they train nearby and asked me to train them, offered me your paper money. It isn't as good as gold, but I have accepted."

"That's great. I bet they're going to be sore and tired after you're done with them."

"They are only fair and require much work, but 'tis my duty to see them trained properly."

She laughed.

He took the packages from her. "Did you buy more books?" He peered into the bags.

"No looking. Late birthday presents for you."

With a glance at the bag by his feet, he patted the pocket of his jeans, which he'd insisted on wearing. "They gave me money for winning today, and I too purchased gifts for you... and a proper tunic and hose to train the whelps, though I do not have boots." He veered toward the stall with the boots, and she knew she had to tell him about one gift.

"Nope, that's one of your gifts. I found boots for you. But the other gift is a surprise, so no more shopping or you'll figure it out too."

He took her hand, twining their fingers together. "As my lady commands." Then he lifted his head, sniffing the air. "Shall we eat? I am powerfully hungry."

"You're always hungry, my bottomless pit. Come on, wait until you see all the choices."

Chapter Sixteen

Even the people around them were impressed with the amount of food Thomas consumed. He'd grinned sheepishly and said he was hungry after the tournament. They were walking back to the car when she spied a tent selling crystals and soaps.

"I want to get Rainbow and the other women a small gift for the upcoming fall solstice. You go on ahead."

He scanned the area before letting go of her hand. "I will not go far. You should have guards when I am not near."

"I'll scream really loud. And we need to get you a phone for times like this—"

Her words were cut off when he swept her into his arms, to the delight of passersby, and kissed her soundly, her arms twining around his neck. Penelope lost herself in him, and the sounds around them faded away until there was only Thomas and his mouth. By the time he put her down, she had to hold on to his forearm for a moment, not trusting her knees not to give out.

She touched a finger to her lips as he chuckled and leaned close to her ear.

"Now all know you are mine, and if they dare lay a finger on you, I will take them into the lists and give them a sound thrashing."

But all she could do was smile like an idiot and nod as he stalked off.

"Wow, your man is hot." The woman running the booth was watching Thomas walk away.

"He certainly is." Once he was out of sight, she turned to the woman and they discussed soaps and crystals.

By the time Penelope had her purchases, an hour had passed. She went in search of Thomas, and was about to turn to her left when a commotion had her following the sound of ringing steel. There was a huge tent set up with a blacksmith working away. He had his shirt off and was banging red-hot steel and then quenching it with water, making it hiss. Mesmerized by the sight, she let out a gasp when he turned. It was Thomas.

He jerked his chin up as if he could smell her, or they were joined by some invisible thread. Their eyes met, and he motioned her over.

"I am fashioning my own bloody blade."

The blacksmith stood close, asking Thomas questions, as did several onlookers, while the women all watched him like he was a juicy cheeseburger and they'd been eating nothing but kale for a month.

"I see that. I'm going to watch. Take as long as you wish."

The blacksmith walked over. "I offered him a blade in exchange for his knowledge. Is he a professor? The things he knows..."

She shook her head. "Something like that. He grew up in England, lived and breathed that history stuff."

"It will take him about sixteen hours to finish the sword. I told him he could come back tomorrow."

Thomas looked so happy that Penelope made a decision on the spot. "That's great. I saw an information booth near the entrance. I'm going to make us a hotel reservation." She called out to Thomas, "I'll be back in a bit."

Absently, he nodded and focused on his work, and she went in search of rooms. Thank goodness he had a tunic and hose to wear tomorrow—she had a dress she'd purchased, and since she always carried a toothbrush and toothpaste with her, they'd manage. Ever since Mildred had eaten spinach quiche one day and walked around all day with spinach stuck in her teeth, Penelope was a bit paranoid, not to mention with all the kissing, she wanted to keep her teeth clean and breath fresh.

Thomas had never been dependent on a woman in all his years. This was vexing, the time, place, and customs he found himself in, but he had earned money today. Winning the tourney, so not so much had changed since his time.

With the money he won and the accord he'd come to with the blacksmith and his brother, a goldsmith, he had what he needed. Thomas looked down at his bare hand. The family ring had been on his finger since he was young, but he had needed the gold from it for the final charm, and he gladly traded it, knowing she would always have a piece of him with her. By tomorrow night he would have a fine sword so he could protect his lady, and... He held up the chain. It was gold, heavy, and he had four charms. A sapphire, a diamond, an emerald, which reminded him of her eyes, and a gold charm in the shape of a unicorn, her favorite beast. 'Twas an unusual betrothal gift, but she did not care for rings, and he thought the charms would be close to her heart, to always remind her of him.

Carefully, he wrapped the necklace back up in the green cloth and put it in his pocket. He would ask her on the beach where they had first met, where she had found him and brought him back to life. So many years he had been alive but never truly lived. Penelope had changed his entire existence, and for the first time in forever, he would forgo duty and stay with her. Not that he had a choice to go back, but if he did...he would stay with her. She was the other half of his heart, and he could not go back to his old life, not without her. She was his world, and he would slay armies if they tried to keep him from her.

"What are you smiling about?"

She came out of the bathing chamber, a towel wrapped around her glorious hair.

"Nothing. Mayhap a surprise for later."

"I love surprises, and speaking of..." She went over to the

bed and handed him two bags.

"I know you know about the boots, but the other...well, I hope I chose wisely."

He took the first bag from her and took out a pair of finely crafted boots. "The leather is so soft." Slipping off his loafers, he tried on the boots, walking over to the tall looking glass to admire them.

"I thank ye, my lady. Such a fine gift."

She stood next to him. "They suit you. I can't wait to see how they look with your new tunic and hose tomorrow." Then she led him back to the bed and pushed him down. "Now close your eyes. No peeking."

He did as she bade him, curious as to what she was so excited about. It took him only a moment to know what she had placed in his outstretched hands.

"They are beautiful." He caressed the daggers, tried them in his boots, and, for the first time since traveling across time, he felt like a new man, better than he was before and whole. Thomas took the blades back out, examining each one. He read the inscription on the one with the emerald in the hilt.

"Who is Dr. Seuss?"

Laughter filled the room. "He's a very smart man."

"Aye, he is." Thomas touched the words. "'You know you're in love when you can't fall asleep because reality is finally better than your dreams.'"

Pulling her close, he inhaled her scent. "'Tis true. My dreams pale compared to you." At last he had come home.

Chapter Seventeen

Penelope had been so busy finishing up projects for work that she'd lost track of time until she heard music fill the house and looked outside to see it was dark. When she came downstairs, she could see what looked like a hundred candles nestled in hurricane jars, flickering on the screened-in porch.

"My lady, will you join me for a stroll on the beach? Then a glass of champagne and your St. Germain?"

Thomas was dressed in his new black tunic and hose, his sword hung at his hips, and he was wearing the second pair of boots she'd insisted he needed, these in black. He looked every inch the medieval knight come to take his damsel away into the night to ravish her. My, wasn't she getting fanciful? It was the effect he had on her—she'd stopped worrying what anyone thought of the two of them, and simply enjoyed the wondrous feelings that came with being helplessly and totally in love.

"I'd love to walk on the beach." She took his offered arm and padded barefoot out to the sand, and as he always did, even at night, he picked her up as effortlessly, as if she were a pillow on the bed, and carried her over the strip of sand that was always hotter than the rest of the beach. Breathless when he put her down, she felt the breeze cooling the back of her neck and ruffling his hair, which was touching his shoulders. Usually he tied it back, but tonight it was loose, and made his gray eyes turn silver in the moonlight.

Other men she had dated either didn't care what she did or weren't interested, but he wanted to know everything about her work, his interest genuine. Tonight she felt like she'd waited her entire life to find him, and hoped one of Rainbow's friends would come through soon with a way to furnish him with identification so he could survive in the modern world. He'd been teaching men and children to fight with swords. A farmer rented them a field he wasn't using in exchange for teaching both his sons to use swords and daggers. People paid well, and she hoped perhaps he could start some kind of sword-fighting school, or when he had papers, maybe teach. After all, he had lived through the time period, so he could tell the students things they wouldn't find anywhere else.

She rinsed off her feet at the outdoor shower, and Thomas brushed off his boots before they settled on the outdoor sofa and he poured her a cocktail. Classical music played softly, and after she'd finished half a glass of her drink, he held out a hand to her.

"Dance with me."

A gull called in the distance as they danced with candles

all around them, softly talking. The song ended, and Thomas poured her another drink, sitting beside her, taking her hands in his.

"I followed the stars to find you. Every step, every choice I made, led me to you." He cleared his throat and knelt at her feet. "I have no gold or home to offer you." Then he pulled his sword and laid it across her lap.

"I give you my blade and my body. I will protect you and cherish you. Loving you throughout time. Will you marry me, Penelope Merriweather?"

Her hands shook as she pulled him up beside her.

"Thomas, I love you with all my heart and soul. I've waited an eternity to find you, but there's something you need to know about me... I have been married before."

"My love, I would expect you to be widowed—you are a grown woman, not a girl. It does not matter."

At that moment, Penelope, who never had regrets, regretted her choices with all her heart. With every fiber of her being, she wished he had been the first. A sigh escaped, and she knew he was not her first love, but he would be her last. If he would still have her once he knew.

"No, I'm not widowed. I've been married and divorced eight times."

He looked out at the water and the stars, and for a minute she thought she'd lost him.

"Look to the sky, my lady. Can you not believe the fates would send me to you? Those men were fools, and if they could not keep you, then it is because the fates decreed you belong to me. But I must tell you: I will never let you go. I will love you until there is no more breath in my body, and then I will love you from beyond."

She was crying so hard that he didn't hear her, and she had to blow her nose.

"Oh, Thomas, I love you with all my heart. There will never be another, only you. If you'll still have me, I'll marry you."

He pulled a cloth-wrapped bundle from underneath a pillow and held out the most beautiful necklace.

"I know ye don't care for rings, so I had this fashioned for you instead."

She held up her hair while he clasped it around her neck, and that was when she noticed what had been bothering her. With a gasp, she took his hand. "Your family ring. Where is it?"

Tucking a lock of hair behind her ear, he said, "I gave it to the goldsmith in exchange for your betrothal necklace." He touched the gold unicorn. "The gold from the band made your favorite beast."

Tears fell again, and he caught each one on his finger, touching it to his lips.

"I know how precious your ring was to you. I didn't need a necklace. You should have kept the ring."

But he shook his head. "Nay, my lady. I wanted you to have it. I no longer need the ring." He looked in her eyes, and she swore she could see his love for her reflected there. "They have been dust for hundreds of years. I must enjoy the life I have now, thanks to you. Before you, I never truly lived, but now I will never waste another day."

She touched the unicorn, the emerald, the sapphire, and the diamond. "I will treasure it always." Then she stroked his cheek, softly pressing her lips to his bare finger. Thomas took her face in his hands, capturing her mouth and branding her for all time. He had taken over every inch of her heart and soul, and she would love him until they were old and gray, strolling together on the beach a little more stooped over, their love growing deeper every year. Life was perfect.

Chapter Eighteen

The next few weeks passed in a bubble of bliss for Penelope. They'd taken several trips to the outer banks and a weekend to the mountains. Yesterday she'd taken Thomas to Fort Fisher, where he peppered the tour guide with a million questions, and, recognizing another history buff—the guy had no idea—they talked and talked while she wandered, content. He had all kinds of questions about the Civil War and the blockade runners that the guide happily answered.

"Tell me again of this aquarium. Have they caught a sea monster? I would like to see the beast that tried to take me down beneath the waves to its lair."

He was driving, the top down, and seeing her medieval man wearing Aviator sunglasses, jeans, and a t-shirt made her smile, because she knew he had the daggers on his person, and the sword was in the trunk. He'd refused to leave it behind, and she'd explained how it really wasn't appropriate to wear it everywhere.

"No sea monsters, but plenty of sharks and fish. Alligators. You'll like gators."

He expertly parked the car and took her hand as they wandered through the exhibits—as she'd predicted, he was fascinated by the alligators, and she told him how every once in a while after a big storm she'd see one ambling along on the beach, which always fascinated anyone around.

"Penelope, look—a monster is in the water with the sharks." Thomas went up to the viewing area next to two young boys, and all three of them pressed their faces to the glass.

Quietly, she said, "That's not a monster. It's a man in a wetsuit and oxygen tank so he can breathe underwater."

Before he could pepper her with questions, she held up a hand. "No, I don't know how it works, but I'm sure we can stop at a dive shop and you can ask all about it."

He grinned and kissed her on the cheek, to the disgust of the little boys next to him.

"You lads will be grateful for a kiss from your lady when you are older."

"Never," said one.

"Girls are gross," said the other, and Penelope had to cover her mouth to keep from laughing at the identical looks of distaste on the boys' faces.

It was late afternoon when they left and found a place for dinner in downtown Wilmington along the river walk. The nights were getting a little cooler, and they sat outside on the water, watching the sun go down.

Afterward, she knew just where to take him. "There's a

great ice cream place up ahead."

Thomas looked down at her heels and pretended to pout. "I love the shoes you wear, but they slow us down when going to have this cream ice you talk about. Shall I carry you?"

"Don't worry, there will be plenty of ice cream for you. As much as I love it when you carry me, we might draw a lot of attention."

He laughed and kissed her fingers. "As my lady wishes."

At the old-fashioned ice cream shop, Thomas must have tasted every flavor. The young guy grinned as he handed him sample after sample.

Thomas nodded at the kid. "Double chocolate brownie, peanut butter swirl, strawberry, and a scoop of mint chocolate chip."

The bowl he handed Thomas was huge. "Want chocolate sauce, whipped cream, and a cherry too?"

Penelope grinned. "He'll take the works." She looked at Thomas. "Trust me, you're going to love whipped cream."

"Anything for you, ma'am?"

"A waffle cone with a scoop of raspberry and a scoop of lemon sorbet."

He handed her the cones, and Thomas paid, whispering to her, "The swordplay lessons pay well."

"Thank you. And don't worry, I'll share mine. I see you eyeing the sorbet."

Hand over his heart, he winked at her. "I would never steal your ice cream...because I know you would share."

"Shall we sit and eat and then we can walk along the river walk?"

"Aye, I like to watch you." Thomas pulled out a chair for her and then got down to the business of eating. In between bites, he asked her about the Merriweather women turning gray early.

"From what I know, it happens to all Merriweather women—some go gray in their twenties, others not until their late forties, but we can't escape it. Well, unless we color it."

"Not like Rainbow." He shuddered. "She is a lovely woman, but blue and purple hair are not as pretty as your sable with silver strands."

"A perfect answer." He'd finished his ice cream and was eyeing the rest of her sorbet. "Go ahead, finish it, and the waffle cone is the best part."

"Penelope? Why do you still have the name Merriweather when you have been married before?"

"It's something we've always done. Family tradition. Will it bother you if I keep it?"

He looked thoughtful for a moment. "I would like you to have my name, but I understand family tradition and duty."

"Could you be any more perfect?" She leaned across the table, and he met her halfway. His lips tasted of sorbet, and that unique scent of him filled her senses, making her wish to hurry home.

Walking along the water, she wasn't paying any attention when she heard the voices.

"Give us your money and your phones and no one gets hurt."

Three men stood in front of them, knives drawn. Thomas pulled her behind him and stepped forward.

"You better back off, dude. We ain't fooling around."

The older one said, "We'll cut you and take your woman."

The change in Thomas was instantaneous. Where before he had been wary but curious, now he balanced on the balls of his feet, and in a flash he had both daggers before him.

One of the guys ran as Thomas laughed.

"Come then, let us see what worthless bastards you both are." He stepped closer, landing a blow to the jaw of the older man with the hilt of his dagger. The guy went down with a groan and didn't get up. At that, the other dropped his knife and ran.

Thomas snorted. "Puny men in this time of yours, Penelope."

Instead of being scared, laughter bubbled up. He was so disgusted that they didn't put up a fight, and she knew she hadn't been in any danger with him there to protect her. He'd put his own body in front of her, for which she loved him even more, if it was possible.

"Take me home and let me show you how grateful I am."

This time he swept her up in his arms. "We will make haste."

Chapter Nineteen

Tomorrow was the fall solstice and the day of the wedding, so today they planned to relax on the beach and enjoy the day. It was going to be a really small wedding. Her friends from her solstice parties and Mildred. Rainbow would officiate on the beach, and that night, under the full moon, Thomas and Penelope would celebrate the solstice and spend the rest of the night learning each other's bodies.

She'd asked him if he wanted to go away for a honeymoon, but he knew she had a deadline, and so they would wait, and when it turned cold in November they would take a Caribbean cruise—if his papers had come through by then. Otherwise, they'd go to the Florida Keys and laze around on the beach.

She opened the freezer to get ice out for their iced tea, and laughed.

"We had three gallons of ice cream in here two days ago.

Where on earth do you put it all? I swear I've gained five pounds these past few weeks."

Thomas peered into the freezer as if he could conjure up more. "'Tis surely enchanted. I heard it call to me late at night."

With a laugh, she hugged him. "Believe me, I can relate."

The tone of her sister's voice was what drew Penelope downstairs, her hair pinned up, makeup done for her wedding. They would be married under the full moon if it didn't rain. The weather guy was predicting intermittent thunderstorms, and while Rainbow said rain on your wedding day was good luck, Penelope hoped it would hold off. Her friends were busy decorating the downstairs in case they had to move the festivities inside.

"How exactly are you going to contribute? Do you expect my sister to take care of you?"

"Mildred! Enough."

But Thomas pulled Penelope close and kissed her cheek. "I have been teaching men to fight, and I am working with the blacksmith to improve his sword-making skills. While I do not bring gold to my marriage with your sister, I am being paid, and I will protect her and cherish her, love her until the end of time."

Mildred thrust a small, tattered book out at Thomas. The

scent of old books met Penelope's nose, and a feeling of dread swept over her. "Even knowing your sister, Josephine, was forced to marry your enemy, Roger DeChartes?"

"Where did you find the book? We looked everywhere." Penelope was furious. Her sister had obviously had the book for a while and waited until the wedding to make a fuss.

Thomas was reading the page Mildred had marked. "Roger always did want my lands." He shut the book with a snap, a look of pain on his face, and said softly, "I cannot aid her. An ocean of time separates us. There was nothing in here of Heath. I must believe he did his best to protect her."

"Well, I'm sure Rainbow could send you back," Mildred said.

"Mildred, she tried," Penelope said. "It didn't work. Why are you doing this today, of all days?"

Her sister was dressed for a funeral, in a severe black pantsuit. "Going for number nine? It's ridiculous. None of your marriages ever last, so what makes this one any different?"

"At least I put myself out there, open up my heart, even if it does get broken. You, you've hit the wall. Let yourself go, become old and closed off."

A sharp pain pierced her heart that her sister couldn't share her joy in this day, couldn't see how happy she was with Thomas, that she had finally found her soul mate.

"So what if I married and failed eight times? At least I gave my whole heart each time."

Mildred snorted. "That's not all you gave."

"Oh shut up." Unable to stay mad at her sister, Penelope laughed, pulling her into a hug. "I know you mean well, but try and be happy for me. It's bad enough Alice is off sailing somewhere and couldn't be here. I need you with me."

Her sister frowned. "He's nice enough, but he doesn't belong with you. I'm sorry, Penelope. I love you, but I'll never support this marriage. I'm going home."

Penelope's heart broke as her sister left. Thomas gathered her in his arms. "She loves you and wants the best for you, my love."

"Let her be cruel. I choose happiness and love with you." She touched his face, blurred by her tears. Thomas caught the a drop before it fell, ruining her makeup.

"No weeping today. Shall I tell you tales of battle and bloodshed?"

It had the desired effect, and she laughed. "Please do. You know I want to know everything about you, and it might keep me from taking your sword and running my sister through."

He chuckled and pulled her on his lap. Her friends had gone outside when Mildred made her entrance, so once Penelope pulled herself together, she went out to tell them her sister wouldn't be participating in the wedding.

"Now, I need a glass of wine, and then I'm going to get dressed."

"Shall I aid you? Those zipper things can be difficult."

"Funny, Thomas." Rainbow patted his arm. "Nice try, though. We'll call you when she's ready." As they went upstairs, she mock-whispered, "I thought seeing a man in a tux was the hottest thing ever, but him, all in black, covered in weapons, is incredibly sexy."

"It is, isn't it?"

Chapter Twenty

The weather was cooperating as Rainbow married them on the beach, Penelope's bright red toes peeking out from under the formfitting white gown.

Thomas turned to her. "I will protect you with my body and my blade, and love you forever. I will spend every day proving myself worthy of your love."

He touched each charm of her necklace shining in the sun as she slid a ring on his finger.

"No matter what, I will stand by your side, be your friend, lover, and companion, your biggest supporter and partner in our many adventures. I swear before all, I will love you until the end of time."

Thomas looked down at his hand. "How? I watched him cut the band to make your charm."

"He still had the stone. The band is new. I couldn't remember what was on it, so I had the date we met and today's date inscribed inside, along with our initials."

He blinked. "I think I've sand in my eye."

Rainbow couldn't keep the grin from her face. "I now pronounce you man and wife. Kiss your bride, Thomas."

He swept her into his arms, and his lips met hers as she wrapped her arms around him, meeting him, telling him with her mouth how much she loved him. They broke apart to cheers from her friends. The only way it could have been better was if Alice and the girls and cranky Mildred had been here.

Clouds blotted out the afternoon sun as they ate and drank, celebrating a new life together, surrounded by friends. By the time the afternoon deepened to evening, Penelope had taken off her dress and was wrapped in a towel when she came back out of the room, ready to celebrate the solstice. Thomas held up his hands.

"You all go. I will stay here and enjoy my cake, watching from a safe distance."

Rainbow and the others laughed as they filed out the door, wrapped in towels, much to the amusement of Thomas. She kissed him soundly and then ran to join them.

Penelope shut the door with a sigh.

"Alone at last with my wife." He held her close, whispering in her ear how they would spend their first night together when the rain started.

"Oh, I love walking on the beach in a storm."

"Then we shall walk." But once outside, he swept her up in his arms. "I love holding you close. I will never let you go."

"I love you too, husband."

The rain smelled salty, the scent of wet sand pleasing as he set her down. They walked under the gentle rain, talking and oblivious to how wet they were. Then Thomas stopped.

"What's that?"

Thunder cracked across the sky, and for the first time, Penelope was afraid of the coming storm.

"Thomas, don't. Let's go inside."

But he had waded out thigh deep, and when the next wave passed, he bent down, coming up with an object. Lightning arced across the sky as he knocked it against a rock, and she saw the glint of metal when the sky lit up again.

"Please leave it." Fear spread through her veins like rushing water, threatening to consume her and pull her under.

Thomas hit the metal against a rock a few more times and turned to her, grinning.

"One of my daggers. I thought it lost forever."

As he held it out to her, he tripped over a piece of

driftwood; in slow motion, she saw three drops of blood fall from his palm. Penelope couldn't move, couldn't speak as energy crackled across her skin.

In a blinding flash of light, time stilled—even the waves seemed to stop as he reached for her, the blood on his palm crimson in the silvery light.

"Penelope, take my hand," he roared over the thunder, and she swore he faded in front of her eyes but...the damned book. Love. It was all that mattered, the one thing she had lived her entire life by, but now? He could go back, save his sister from a terrible man, put right wrongs that should have never occurred in the first place.

"You can save them."

He took a step forward, even as the storm intensified. "Nay. Take my hand."

Knowing it would not work, she reached out, but her hand went through his, and he roared.

"Don't take me from her."

And in that moment, their hands touched, fingers intertwined. Tears streamed down her face, and she knew what she must do. Gently she disentangled their hands, stepping back, sacrificing her love so he could save his family. Duty and responsibility—they were as much a part of him as his love for her.

"Please let him go back to the exact moment he arrived. This is all I ask." She reached out again, and this time, her hand did not touch a flesh-and-blood man, but a ghost. "I will love you until we meet again."

He tried to step forward, but was held in place, reaching out for her, a look of anguish on his face. "I vow, I will love you for all my days and haunt you for all of yours. I will never let you go, Penelope."

The flash of light sent her flying backward.

Chapter Twenty-One

"Pittypat, wake up. I've had awful news. I've been trying to call you for hours and hours."

Slowly she opened her eyes to see Mildred leaning over her.

"Thomas?"

Penelope sat up, waiting for the dizziness to subside.

"Oh my goodness, what happened to your hand?"

Frowning, Penelope held up her right hand, and there on her palm was a tiny black mark in the center that kind of looked like a sideways heart. She coughed and got to her feet, everything flooding back.

"Oh, Thomas."

"You keep saying that. Where is your new husband? Lost him already?"

She burst into tears, fleeing the words until she stood waist deep in the surf, letting the ocean wash away the tears.

The pain would be her constant companion for the rest of her life.

Had he made it home?

"Pittypat? What on earth is wrong with you? I've been trying to tell you. There's been an accident."

"I know."

"But how? I've been trying to call you for ages."

She looked at her sister, a terrible feeling threatening to pull her under. "What bad news?"

"Alice and her husband were lost at sea. The storm took the sailboat. They recovered the bodies a few hours ago. Thank goodness the girls were with his parents, but they can't look after them." Mildred frowned. "Alice gave them to you. I don't know why. I would make a much better parent. Just look at you, wading out into the ocean. You obviously slept on the beach, and your new husband has already run off. You're a terrible choice for the girls."

The words finally penetrated Penelope's brain, and the next wave took her under. She tumbled over and over, scraping the bottom, knowing that if she took a deep breath, it would all be over, the pain would stop, and she would find Thomas waiting for her. Penelope was about to let the ocean have her when the rest of Mildred's words sank in. She was now responsible for three young girls. No way did Penelope want them growing up with her sister, so she dragged herself to her feet, spluttering and coughing, and trudged out of the water.

"Thomas didn't leave me. He went back to his own time. I let him go. I'm not always selfish. That's all I'm saying to you about him. From this moment forward, you are never to utter his name. If you do, I will never speak to you again."

Wringing out her hair, she looked to the house. "Come on, there's lots to do to get the house ready for three girls."

"Fine. I was only trying to help. Melinda is fifteen. She's going to be a handful. You'll need help."

But Penelope had already tuned her sister out, her thoughts of Thomas, fervently hoping he had made it back in time to save his family, and that someday, when it was her time, he'd be waiting.

Tomorrow was the funeral. Penelope had to hide her grief over losing Thomas, and be strong now that she was responsible for three girls. She vowed to love them as her own and make sure they never forgot their parents.

Rainbow joined her on the beach. "How are you holding up?"

"Do you think it worked? That he went back to the right time?" She looked down at her red toes, remembering how much he like the color.

"Haven't you looked?"

Penelope shook her head, listening to the gulls call to each other. "I've been afraid to. What if I gave up my one true love and soul mate and sent him to another time, and he died when he got back and couldn't save his brother and sister? I don't think I could live with myself."

Rainbow looked at her with those wise golden eyes. "I've known you a long time—you're one of the most fearless people I know. You've never been afraid of the truth. Now go on and look. I'll be here, whatever you find out."

Penelope's heart twitched as she hugged her friend and Rainbow added, "But I believe the universe recognized the ultimate sacrifice you made and sent him back to the moment he left. Call me later, sugar."

The rest of the day, Penelope scoured the used bookstore, made phone calls, even international, to find out, and finally, a professor at a university in Scotland got back to her with news.

"Right, Thomas Wilton of Oakwick Manor. His half-sister made an advantageous marriage—his half-brother took over the wool business, and Thomas, he died in battle, never married. Is that what you were looking for?"

She had to clear her throat as she touched the charms. "Thank you. It's exactly what I was looking for. I can't thank you enough." Penelope called one of the women from her circle and commissioned a quilt for the professor as a thank-you.

But he'd gotten one thing wrong...Thomas had married, to her.

Underneath the Holden Beach sun, as the gulls circled and the waves crashed, they'd professed their love. He'd kept his vow, and she would hers. One day, no matter how much it hurt now, someday they would be together again. Penelope knew it as she knew there would always be air to breathe.

A walk on the beach and a conversation with Thomas gave her strength to face the funeral today. While she knew he couldn't hear her, had been gone for hundreds of years, she truly believed he was somewhere listening, watching over her. She wiped a tear from her eyes as she came to the spot with the higher dunes, where she'd found him back in June.

A raven landed on the sand, close enough that if she'd knelt down, she could touch the bird. The black bird cocked its head and hopped toward her, dropping a tiny piece of black cloth. Joy filled her heart. He was okay, and someday they'd find each other again. Soul mates always did. It was the waiting that would be the worst. Thank goodness she would have her nieces to care for—they would ease the ache that pounded her battered heart day and night.

"I love you, Thomas."

The bird cawed and took flight, disappearing into the sun.

Chapter Twenty-Two

Epilogue—Elsewhere

Penelope woke, rubbing her heart. She felt funny. What had she been doing? Lucy. Her dear niece had gone missing. Penelope was sure that slimy boyfriend of hers was behind what had happened. The sound of a violin had her looking down as if from a great distance. It was a funeral: Mildred, Melinda, and Charlotte were there, as were Rainbow and all of the ladies from her circle. Who had died?

The thought brought her close, and she saw it was her. Of course, she'd been outside walking on the beach, talking to Thomas, when she felt the searing pain and then peace. There was another sound, and when she looked through the mist, she saw Lucy. She wasn't dead, she had gone back in time, found her own soul mate, and, well...

She looked down again. Melinda and Charlotte were in

for the trips of a lifetime.

A hand on her arm made her heart flutter.

"My love. I've waited over seven hundred years for you."

"Thomas."

He caught her in his arms as she ran to him. It was as if the years melted away. She saw herself, younger and carefree, reflected in his eyes, and their love for each other burned so brightly that she swore it would outshine the sun and the stars. The kiss was even better than she'd remembered, searing her from her lips to her toes.

"We will look after them together, my love. Do what we can to keep your nieces safe."

"I know we will. Now kiss me again, darling." They had eternity.

Soul mates always do.

Books by Cynthia Luhrs

Listed in the correct reading order

THRILLERS
There Was A Little Girl
When She Was Bad
When She Was Good - Coming end 2017
Crimson Pool - 2018

TIME TRAVEL SERIES
A Knight to Remember
Knight Moves
Lonely is the Knight
Merriweather Sisters Medieval Time Travel Romance
Boxed Set Books 1-3
Darkest Knight
Forever Knight
First Knight
Thornton Brothers Medieval Time Travel Romance
Boxed Set Books 1-3
Last Knight
The Merriweather Sisters and Thornton Brothers
Medieval Time Travel Romance Boxed Set Series Books
1-7

My One and Only Knight
Beyond Time - Coming Summer 2017

COMING 2017 - 2018
Falling Through Time
Lost in Time
A Moonlit Knight
A Knight in Tarnished Armor
Crimson Pool
The Ghost and Miss Gray

THE SHADOW WALKER GHOST SERIES
Lost in Shadow
Desired by Shadow
Iced in Shadow
Reborn in Shadow
Born in Shadow
Embraced by Shadow
The Shadow Walkers Books 1-3
The Shadow Walkers Books 4-6
Entire Shadow Walkers Boxed Set Books 1-6

A JIG THE PIG ADVENTURE
(Children's Picture Books)

Beware the Woods
I am NOT a Chicken!

August 2016 – December 2017 My Favorite Things
Journal & Coloring Book for Book Lovers

Want More?

Thank you for reading my book. Reviews help other readers find books. I welcome all reviews, whether positive or negative and love to hear from my readers. To find out when there's a new book release, please visit my website http://cluhrs.com/ and sign up for my newsletter. Please like my page on Facebook. http://www.facebook.com/cynthialuhrsauthor
Without you dear readers, none of this would be possible.

P.S. Prefer another form of social media? You'll find links to all my social media sites on my website.

Thank you!

About the Author

Cynthia Luhrs writes time travel because she hasn't found a way (yet) to transport herself to medieval England where she's certain a knight in slightly tarnished armor is waiting for her arrival. She traveled a great deal and now resides in the colonies with three tiger cats who like to disrupt her writing by sitting on the keyboard. She is overly fond of shoes, sloths, and tea.

Also by Cynthia: There Was a Little Girl, When She Was Bad, and the Shadow Walker Ghost Series.

Made in the USA
Las Vegas, NV
26 March 2021